I0518134

STAY IN TOUCH

Sign up for Aria's newsletter to keep up with new paranormal romance and urban fantasy releases, win bookish giveaways, receive opportunities for advance review copies, and more.

ONE NIGHT WITH A BEAR

One night with a bear becomes so much more...

When Dr. Jade Barnes impulsively stops at a bar before leaving for a four-month archaeology dig, she spends a single night with a stranger, not even learning his last name. When she slips away the next morning, she doesn't realize she isn't leaving alone.

When they meet again, Cody surprises her by how well he takes the news of impending fatherhood. There are further surprises awaiting, like the fact he's a bear-shifter. Initially that terrifies her, but she soon appreciates his strength and protectiveness when someone targets her for an unknown, but nefarious, purpose.

Cody can protect her body, but it's her heart in danger when the stubborn bear-shifter makes it known he's going to claim her as his mate, and he's not above using every dirty trick he knows—including killer foot massages and kisses that make her whole body tingle.

Genuine and true love is so rare that when you encounter it in any form, it's a wonderful thing, to be utterly cherished in whatever form it takes.

— *GWENDOLINE CHRISTIE*

---

*J*ade braced herself as the gawky young man who'd been eyeing her for the last twenty minutes seemed to work up the nerve to approach. She had come to the bar hoping for some companionship, but this guy had to be at least ten years her junior, and he reminded her of the kids she taught at the university every day. There was no way it was going to happen, and she'd hope that by ignoring him, it would take care of itself. No such luck.

He sat down at the bar beside her, all fake confidence and swagger, slamming his empty glass onto the bar. That earned him an annoyed look from the bartender, and she barely bit back a giggle when the kid flinched. He wasn't quite the stud he pretended to be. It softened her slightly toward him. Not enough to actually accept any of his overtures, but she'd try to be gentle with her letdown.

"Hey, how you doing?"

She managed a neutral nod, thinking he sounded so much like that old character on "Friends." What was his name? Joey, that was the one. It had been years since she'd seen that show, and she had a feeling this kid had never seen it unless he'd watched it on Netflix. "I'm fine." She didn't inquire about him, hoping to cut short the conversation.

Apparently, the kid just didn't get subtlety. "May I buy you a drink?"

She looked down at her mostly full Bloody Mary. "I'm good."

He was starting to look shaky, and she was amused when he shot a glance over his shoulder. She could well imagine his friends at the table were giving him a thumbs-up or other signs of encouragement, delusional young men that they were.

"Do you come here often?"

Jade shrugged. "Upon occasion. It's close to work." Which also meant it was close to the university, which was a downside. She really had picked the wrong bar this evening if she'd hoped to meet someone to take home.

"Where do you work?" His eyes gleamed with excitement suddenly. "Do you work at that strip club across the street?"

She let out a genuine laugh as she gave her curvy body a rueful glance. She imagined there would certainly be a market for curvy strippers, but that was outside her field of expertise. "No, not at all. I work at the university."

The bartender had brought him a fresh glass, but he showed no sign of taking his beer back to his table. "What do you do there?"

"I'm a professor of archaeology."

He suddenly looked slightly ashen. "A professor?"

She gave him a smile, though it didn't reach her eyes. "Yes. Didn't I have you last semester?" She was certain she hadn't, but she was hoping to emphasize the age difference to the young man without having to brutally shoot him down.

He gulped his beer, looking like he might choke on it for a

moment. "No, I don't think so. I haven't taken an archae-ology class yet."

"You go to the university then?"

He nodded again. "Yeah. First year," he mumbled, as though embarrassed by the revelation.

She winced slightly, having pegged him at least a few years older than that. It was a good thing she wasn't a cougar. She couldn't help frowning at the glass of beer in his hand. "Aren't you a bit young for that then?" She asked the question quietly, so as not to rouse the bartender's interest. He was busy with the group that had recently entered anyway, and they looked as out-of-place as she felt tonight. In their leather and denim, they seemed to scream biker gang, and she wondered how they'd ended up at this bar.

He shrugged, looking defensive. "I'm twenty-one."

"Of course you are," she said dryly.

The kid stopped making any further attempts to pick her up after that. He took his drink and slunk back to his table, where she was certain his friends commiserated with him, and perhaps pointed out he'd had a lucky break by avoiding the old broad. No, those kids probably didn't use the word broad at all. She didn't know exactly what they would call her, and she was fine with that. She didn't aspire to be the cool professor, and she didn't much care about what was hip or popular among the younger kids.

Wow, she was starting to sound like an old curmudgeon. Here she was, only thirty-two, and already set in her ways. She might as well embrace spinsterhood and buy at least ten cats if she kept on this path.

The idea of packing up ten cats to take with her to her next dig site was a ludicrous idea, and she almost giggled aloud. She would have if she hadn't looked up at just the right moment to see a new person entering the bar. She could tell right away he was part of the biker group, or at least meeting them, since he wore sinfully tight jeans, a crisp white t-shirt, and a leather vest. It wasn't his outfit that garnered her attention though.

It was, bluntly, his smoking hot body to start with. He had muscular thighs, and she was certain his stomach would be flat as a washboard with a well-defined six-pack. She found herself idly wondering if he would have a lot of chest hair or just a little bit. She decided he'd be on the slightly hairy side, but she didn't know why she thought that.

Her gaze swept higher, and her eyes locked with his. His eyes were the shade of the ocean at midday and fringed by thick blond lashes. He had scruff on his cheeks, and his hair was slightly overgrown. He had the careless renegade look down perfectly, but she was convinced it wasn't an affectation. She doubted he had spent hours going for the look. Rather, it had just occurred naturally for him.

She was embarrassed when her nipples hardened against the lace of her bra, and she had to resist the self-conscious urge to cross her arms over her chest to hide proof of her sudden arousal.

She held her breath as she waited to see if he would approach her, and she refused to acknowledge the wave of disappointment that swept through her when he turned away from her to meet his friends instead. Clearly, the interest had been one-sided. Feeling glum, she finished the rest of her drink and dropped a few bills on the bar. This was turning out to be a disaster of a night, and she really should head home to get some sleep since her flight left early the next morning.

She was just about to climb off the stool when she realized he was standing behind her. She turned slowly, looking over her shoulder and up at him. Way up. He was a big, solid man, and though she was curvy, she had a feeling he could pick her up easily. The thought might have alarmed her from anyone else, but the idea of him doing it only excited her.

"Leaving already?" It was a rough growl more than syllables.

She shrugged a shoulder. "I have an early flight."

"Join me for a drink first." It wasn't exactly an invitation. It was more like a demand coated in velvet, but his body language made it clear he wasn't letting her go just yet.

If she hadn't been so attracted to him, she would have found his attitude insufferable. She normally would anyway, but there was just something about him that made her want to comply. He didn't need to know that though. "You're awfully bossy."

His chiseled lips twitched, and he inclined his head. "Guilty as charged."

She didn't resist when he took her hand and led her to a table in the corner, one that would give them some privacy. Her heart raced at the touch of his hand, and she found it difficult to draw in a deep breath. She was either really attracted to him, or she was about to have a pulmonary embolism.

They sat together, and she realized neither one of them had ordered drinks. Apparently, that didn't matter, because the bartender quickly arrived with drinks for both of them. It was the first time she'd seen him leave the bar all night. He usually made the patrons come to him. Was he responding to the stranger's commanding presence too?

"Another Bloody Mary for the lady, and your usual, Cody."

As the bartender stepped away, her eyes widened with surprise. "You're a regular here?"

He took a sip of his beer before responding. "Would that surprise you?"

She shrugged. "It's more of a college hangout than a biker bar."

He grinned. "Yes, it is. The bartender's my nephew though."

She looked back at the young man behind the bar before glancing at him again. "He can't be much younger than you are."

He shook his head. Cody was what the bartender called him. Cody shook his head. He looked like a Cody.

She was mentally rambling like a moron.

"I'm about ten years older than he is. I was a late baby and a big surprise for my mom and dad, and all my brothers are older than me. After six boys already, they thought they were done, but along came me. Then my oldest brother had my nephew a few years after I was born."

She took a sip of the Bloody Mary, finding it just as perfect as the last one. "So your mom had seven boys? How many girls?"

"None. Girls aren't born in our family very often, for some reason." He shrugged. "My nephew Kade and his mate...wife bucked that trend though. They have a little girl and another one on the way."

She found the idea of such a large family fascinating, but that was probably because she'd grown up as an only child. Like Cody, she'd been a surprise late baby for her parents, though neither one of them had really ever wanted to have children. Her mother had been forty-seven when she was born, and far too old and set in her ways to understand or indulge a young child.

Madeline Barnes had happily entrusted her care to the nanny and gone about her life as usual. Frank Barnes had been just as absorbed in his own academic career, and she hadn't seen much of her parents at all until she was older, had learned her manners, and knew to always be quiet and polite around them, and never behave like a child. It must have been amazing to grow up with so many siblings, even if they were older than Cody.

She was envious for a moment, and she nearly confessed her own wish to have a large family—a desire that seemed less likely as the years passed. While she could conceivably have children for at least ten more years, she wasn't certain she wanted to have them that close together. And discussing the family she wanted with a potential one-night stand seemed like the best way to send him running, which she didn't want.

For that matter, the prospect of having any children was pretty dim at the moment. She couldn't seem to find a man who interested her or could put up with her own eccentricities for longer than a few weeks. She'd been in such a long dry spell that it was practically a drought, and that was unlikely to change in the next four months when she was at the dig site. She'd be surrounded by eager young students, and perhaps a colleague or two, but no one who made her heart race the way this man did. "What was it like growing up with all those brothers?"

Cody shrugged. "They were a lot older than me, like I said, so I think I annoyed the hell out of them as I tagged along. They were good about watching out for me though, and we're still close. We're closer now that I'm an adult and no longer that annoying little brother."

"What were you like as a kid?"

"Always in trouble." He made the admission with a charming grin.

It provoked a smile of her own in response. "Oddly enough, I imagine you're telling me the truth."

He gave her a cocky grin. "I don't lie."

"Ever?"

He shrugged. "I try not to."

She snorted. "Everybody tells lies. Just the little ones maybe, like if I asked you do these pants make my butt look fat, you're going to say no, of course not. We both know they do, but I don't care because they're comfortable." Skinny jeans weren't necessarily an invention intended for women of her size, but she didn't care. She liked them, so she wore them.

There was a new level of heat in his eyes when he raked his gaze over her again. "Honestly, I can't see your butt from here, but from what I remember as you got off the barstool, it was a luscious ass, and those jeans are perfect for it."

She almost choked on the drink in her mouth, not having expected that. "You're a smooth one."

"I'm just being honest. You asked me what I thought of your ass, and I'm telling you it's about the best one I've ever seen."

She blushed like a schoolgirl, which was embarrassing in itself. "Actually, I mentioned my jeans, and not my ass. I mean I wasn't asking for your opinion of my ass."

Cody sipped his beer before responding. "I guess you can have my opinion for free then. The ass is spectacular, as is the rest of the package. You're a beautiful woman, and I don't even know your name."

She giggled before abruptly cutting off the juvenile sound. "I'm sorry. We haven't been formally introduced. I heard the bartender call you Cody, but I forgot to give you my name." She held out her hand, unsurprised when she found his fingers and palm rough from hard work. It was a pleasant feel and a nice contrast to the usual hands she shook in her daily academic life. "I'm Dr. Jade Barnes."

He looked impressed. "You're a doctor, huh? I've got this spot I'd like you to look at." His eyes twinkled as they darted down to his lap before looking up at her again.

She shook her head. "Sorry, but that's the wrong kind of

doctor. I have a PhD in archaeology, and I'm a professor at the university."

"I still have a spot I'd like you to look at."

She couldn't hold in a laugh. "I still say you're a smooth talker, whether or not you're being honest."

"I assure you I'm being completely honest about the spot I'd like you to see. You have some spots I'd like to see too. See, touch, and taste." This time, there was no teasing his expression. "Do you want to get out of here?"

Did she? There was hardly a space between him asking and her answering. "Yes, very much." She had come to the bar this evening with the half-formed idea of picking up someone if the opportunity arose, since she was sure to be out of social contact for the next few months, starting tomorrow.

It had been more than a year since the last time she'd been with a man, and that had been a brief, disastrous relationship. She wasn't after a relationship. This was just sex, and though she wasn't accustomed to one-night stands, not having one since college, she decided to go for it tonight. What was the worst that could happen?

Immediately, she realized he could be a serial killer, but she quickly discarded that notion. She couldn't explain it, but she trusted Cody. Perhaps it was because she believed he really was an honest man, or perhaps it was because she wanted him so badly that she was fooling herself. Whatever it was, she barely had any second thoughts as she followed him out of the bar and across the road to a hotel bearing the logo of a national chain.

She rented the room, uncertain of his financial status. That didn't matter to her anyway, especially for just one night, but she wasn't positive he could afford it. She supposed that was a snobbish assumption, and the kind of judgment her parents would make, but she shrugged it off.

She had good intentions, and even if she found out he had filed bankruptcy ten times in a row, it didn't matter for what she wanted from him. Just sex, she reminded herself as she took the key card, and they walked together to the elevator.

As soon as they stepped inside, she realized the compartment felt smaller than usual. Cody had a way of dominating the space and seeming to suck up all the oxygen. That was the only explanation for her sudden breathlessness. Either that, or his proximity. Either way, it was his fault.

She half-expected him to touch her in the elevator, even in just a casual way, but he kept his hands to himself and stayed on his side of the elevator, much to her disappointment. She was too old for a grope session in the elevator, but it suddenly seemed like a fun idea with this man.

Fortunately, they were on the third floor, so the ride took only a few seconds. The desk clerk had given them a room near the elevator, and she reminded herself to give him a large tip if she saw him again. Perhaps he recognized two horny people in desperate need of each other and had done his best to make it easy on them.

More likely, it had simply been the next available room, but she rather liked the idea of thinking there were outside forces at work that had arranged this night for them. It was a fanciful thought for a professor who didn't believe in anything she couldn't see, touch, taste, or hear. She didn't believe in fate, but a man like Cody made her want to.

The room was nicely furnished, if average and nondescript. It had everything they needed, which was basically the bed.

As soon as the door closed behind them, Cody reached for her. All the anticipation of the evening rushed through her, leaving her head spinning as he put his arms around her. He was even more solid than she had guessed, and it was like embracing a stone pillar as he held her against him. He smelled like pine and something uniquely male, and his lips were softer than she had guessed when they molded to hers. His stubble was scratchy, but in a pleasant way, and she opened her mouth to yield to his questing tongue.

He kissed like he did everything else, in a forceful and commanding way. He demanded her submission, and she had no trouble granting it. It was completely unlike her, but she surrendered to the impulse, allowing Cody to take the lead.

They continued kissing as he moved her inexorably backward toward the bed, and she didn't even realize he was maneuvering her that way until her knees hit the mattress, causing her to fall onto her bum on the soft mattress. She let out a small squeal of surprise, but he quickly swallowed the sound as he deepened the kiss. He twined his hands in her blonde hair, holding her tightly against him as though afraid she would slip away if given the chance. She had no intention of going anywhere, and to prove it, she clung to his shoulders, urging him closer.

He seemed to have magic fingers and had soon unbuttoned her top and pushed it off her shoulders. In contrast, hers were fumbling with the zipper on his vest. It should have been an easy task, yet she couldn't seem to manage it.

"Leave it," he growled, taking her hand away. It was an inpatient gesture, but she intuited it came from his desperate need for her, rather than him being annoyed at her difficulty with removing his garment.

Cody stood up for a moment, seeming to be reluctant to part from her. She felt the same way, and she took advantage of him stripping off his clothes to do the same with her own. It was a bit unnerving to get naked with a stranger, but as Cody returned to her, gathering her into his arms again, she realized he didn't feel like a stranger. It was different to have such an instant connection with someone, and she tried to shrug it off, assuring herself it was just sex. That's all she wanted or needed from him.

Cody pushed her back onto the bed, his mouth finally wandering from hers to move down her body. He took one firm nipple into his mouth, sucking gently while his hand cupped her other breast. His fingers glided around her nipple, tugging intermittently, and she moaned at the sensation. She was already more excited than she'd ever been with another man, and she could only imagine how it would be when they actually had sex. She couldn't wait to feel him inside her—on the other hand, she was in no hurry to speed up the foreplay either. Especially since his mouth was so good at what it was doing.

That mouth decided to travel farther down, and her stomach fluttered with excitement as his tongue trailed over her abdomen before moving lower, and he paused at the apex of her thighs. She shivered when he buried his face against her, breathing in her scent. She was convinced that's what he was doing, and it seemed strange, but also sexy as hell.

"Mine," he said in a gruff voice before his mouth covered her. His tongue slid between her folds, and he immediately sought out her neglected clit. Jade grasped handfuls of his overly long hair, pinning him closer to her body. He chuckled against her core, making her lower half twitch, and she arched against him in a demanding fashion.

Cody didn't seem to mind complying with her request, and he began to lick faster. His tongue probed all of her parts, learning everything about her sheath and soon bringing her to the edge of orgasm. He held her there for a moment, not allowing her to slip over. He stopped moving his tongue and stopped sucking.

"Please," she whimpered. With a small laugh, he darted

out his tongue and flicked it under the hood of her clit, which sent her flying completely over the edge.

As she was coming down from her orgasm, she was vaguely aware of him moving off the bed again to retrieve something from his pants. As she heard the foil packet tear, she realized he had gone for a condom. Thankfully he had the foresight to use one, because she was so caught up in the bliss of the moment that she would have happily taken him inside her and not even thought about the consequences until much later.

It should have been a wake-up call, but she was too far immersed in how she was feeling and how much she wanted Cody to worry about how deeply in she was already. Instead, she held out her arms and welcomed him back to her, taking the condom from him and sliding it on his shaft herself. Her eyes widened slightly as she realized just how large he was, and she gulped quietly. It was a good thing she wasn't a virgin, or this never would have worked.

"Are you ready for me, baby?" He seemed to ask the question through gritted teeth, as though he were in pain. Perhaps he was, finding it as difficult to hold back as she was.

She nodded. "More than ready. Are you?"

He looked to be in pain, as though her question had caused him physical suffering. "I was ready from the moment I smelled you across the bar."

She frowned at that. "Do I stink?"

He chuckled. "No, not at all. You smell amazing."

It was a strange compliment, but she was more than happy to take it, just like his cock. Still holding it in her hands, she guided him to her opening before letting go. She moved her hands to his back and wrapped her thighs around his waist as he sank into her. They began to thrust against each other, slowly at first, but soon caught up in the passion of the moment.

The pace of his thrusts increased, and she moved her hands to his buttocks, digging in her nails lightly to encourage him to take all of her. She had been concerned about his size, but once he was inside her, it was as though they were made to fit each other. She wanted more of him, so she increased the pace of her hips, and he responded. Soon, they were clinging to each other as they orgasmed simultaneously. She'd never done that with a lover before, and to achieve it with what was essentially a one-night stand with someone she barely knew was a strange turn of events.

Somehow, she was unsurprised though. It just felt right with Cody. Everything felt right with him, which was slightly alarming, since this was only one night. Just sex, she reminded herself as they indulged in more. It was a long night, and she was going to be exhausted on her plane ride tomorrow, but she couldn't find it in herself to care or worry about the practicalities at the moment. She was too absorbed in Cody.

*S*ometime near dawn, they fell asleep, and he was still inside her. That felt right too, but it proved awkward when she woke an hour later, the alarm on her watch alerting her that it was time to get up and get ready for her flight. She still had to go home and grab her bag, and she didn't have time to shower or to have a long, drawn-out goodbye with her one-night stand. She couldn't imagine it was Cody's style anyway, and he would probably appreciate her slipping quietly away into the night without the fuss of a morning-after postmortem of the night before.

Gingerly, she pulled away from him, squirming across the bed until she could swing free and get up. She waited to see if he had awakened, but he was snoring softly. She had worn him out, but as a wave of exhaustion swept over her, she knew it was a mutual effect they'd had on each other. She was definitely going to sleep most of the day on the plane.

She dressed quickly, finding as many of her clothes as possible. The location of her bra was a mystery, so she left it behind. She felt like she was sneaking out, and she supposed she was, but she was saving them both any awkwardness. That was how these things worked, right? She hadn't had a one-night stand since college, but she remembered the awkwardness of the morning after, when the guy had offered her breakfast he clearly didn't want to fix, and she hadn't been able to get dressed fast enough.

She'd regretted that night, but she was certain she wouldn't regret anything about the one she'd spent with Cody, except perhaps the duration. One night didn't seem like nearly enough, but there were no other alternatives. She still didn't know his last name, and she was going to be out of town for four months. By the time she returned, he would have forgotten all about her, and she was certain she would forget about him by then too.

After all, it was just sex.

---

2

*J*ade was so tired that the words on the form blurred for a moment, forcing her to blink to clear her vision.

She had been back in Seattle for eighteen hours now, and during that time, she'd inventoried all the finds from the dig, began the process of sorting out who would receive what, and called her doctor for a long-overdue appointment. She'd also managed to squeeze in a few hours of sleep, but it hadn't been enough. It never felt like enough these days.

She jumped in surprise when the nurse called her name, having only completed about half of the form. It was simply an update for information, so she was able to quickly sort through it and scrawl her name as she got awkwardly to her feet. She recognized Marla, who had been Dr. Grayson's nurse last time she'd been in for her annual gynecological exam.

She smiled at the older woman. "How are you, Marla?"

"I'm doing well. How about you, Dr. Barnes?"

Jade shrugged, looking down ruefully. "As well as can be expected, I guess."

Marla led her through the check-in process, and Jade winced when she saw how many pounds had been added to the scale since her last weigh-in at her annual physical. She hadn't even looked at a scale while in Africa, since they weren't easy to come by—especially on a closed archaeological dig carefully guarded by private security and the government.

After taking her blood pressure in a separate room, Marla led her into an exam room and helped her climb onto the table. Jade felt awkward needing the assistance, but she was still getting used to the changes in her body.

"First thing's first, Dr. Barnes. How far along are you?"

"Four months," said Jade, resting a hand on her burgeoning belly. It had been a shock when she'd started feeling ill at the dig site, and the illness hadn't gone away.

At first, she'd thought it was food poisoning, or an inadvertent exposure to a contaminant in the local water supply, but soon enough, she'd realized the nausea came mostly in the mornings. She felt better after vomiting, and when her breasts became tender, a light bulb went off in the back of her brain.

Since she'd been on a tiny island off the coast of Africa, there hadn't been an opportunity to test, let alone see a doctor, but less than a month after her night with Cody, she had known she was pregnant. The speed at which she'd developed symptoms had been surprising, so she wasn't offended when Marla gave her a skeptical look.

She did have a larger tummy than even she would have expected, but she'd never been pregnant before, so it might be perfectly normal for the women in her family to pop early. Her mother would never have discussed such things with her, so she had no clue about familial history.

"Are you certain it's only four months?"

Jade frowned, but nodded. "I'm positive. It can only be

four months. It was only one time, and it was the first time in a long time."

The nurse made a note on the chart before opening the cabinet door above her head. She removed a gown and a cup, which she placed on the edge of the counter. "We'll need a sample, and Dr. Grayson will be in soon."

She thanked Marla as she climbed down from the table to visit the bathroom connected to the room. She stripped as quickly as possible and provided the sample before returning to the exam room. Jade had just lumbered back onto the bed when the door opened, and Dr. Grayson entered. She was a petite black woman close to Jade's age, and usually had a friendly smile on her face. It was absent today, replaced by a look of concern.

She shook Jade's hand before going to the sink to wash hers and donning gloves. "Have you seen a doctor at all, Jade?"

Jade shook her head. "I was on a dig site when I realized I was pregnant, and civilization was hours away. I haven't seen a doctor yet. I haven't even had prenatal vitamins." She'd had regular vitamins, so she had doubled up on those, at least until she ran out. When she told the doctor that, the other woman nodded.

"That was a smart thing to do, and it would have been good timing. Prenatal vitamins are important for the entire pregnancy, but folic acid is particularly crucial during the first few weeks, when the neural tubes are developing. It sounds like you did the best you could under the circumstances."

Jade nodded, having set out to do everything to protect the baby that she could after discovering its existence. She hadn't even questioned the idea of keeping her child and raising it. "It was quite a surprise, but it just wasn't practical to leave the dig site."

She couldn't have torn herself away unless it was a true emergency. Having been one of the few government-sanctioned teams onsite, she and her group of students and colleagues had dug enthusiastically into the recently discovered Sumerian outpost, finding a plethora of interesting artifacts, many of which still needed identification and would likely stir debate among scholarly circles on their intended purpose.

She had another reason for not leaving the site, and that came in the form of Julian Sig. Ostensibly, he was an archaeologist, and while he possessed the credentials, he didn't have the same academic bent as most of the people she knew. She suspected he had been raiding sites and selling artifacts for years, so she and her team had been determined not to allow his people to get their hands on anything if they could help it.

They had worked diligently all day, and often into the night, to ensure they found whatever they could in the timeframe they had and kept Sig's people away from their part of the site.

"Let's get a picture of the baby first, and then I'll do a physical exam. Your blood pressure looks good, and there's no protein in your urine, so you appear to be very healthy, which is a good sign."

When Jade laid back on the bed, she saw the way Dr. Grayson's eyes widened when she saw her tummy as she walked over to the corner to retrieve the portable ultrasound machine, bringing it close to the exam table. "I think Marla must have written it down wrong. She recorded you at four months along."

"No, that has to be right."

The doctor opened the snaps on the front of the gown, leaving it pooled modestly to cover her breasts while exposing her bare tummy. "This will be a little cold." A second later, she squirted gel on her skin, making Jade wince at the coolness.

The wand pressed against her stomach a moment later, and the sound of a rapidly beating heart filled the room. Jade frowned when she realized there was a strange echo. She had no medical training, but it didn't sound quite right. "Is something wrong with the baby?"

Dr. Grayson was frowning, but she looked up and met Jade's gaze. "Actually, there's two of them."

She let out a harsh and shaky sigh, not prepared to hear that news. The idea of raising one baby by herself was daunting, but two was suddenly impossible. She knew she could do it, but it was a frightening prospect.

She didn't even know if she'd be raising them alone, but since she had no idea how to find Cody again, she had to brace herself for the possibility that she was going to be the single mother of twins. It required an adjustment in her thinking.

Abruptly, she realized Dr. Jade's expression of concern hadn't faded. "Is there something wrong with the babies?"

After a moment, the doctor shook her head. "No, there's nothing wrong, but you're farther along than you thought."

Jade opened her mouth to argue, but instead asked, "How far along am I?"

"You're about six months into the pregnancy."

Flabbergasted, Jade just stared at her for a moment. "That's impossible. I didn't have sex with anyone six months ago."

The doctor turned the screen in her direction, as though it would make a difference to Jade's comprehension. "I can tell by the length of the femur and the general development of the twins that you're at least six months along, dear."

Jade's head spun, but she stopped arguing as she stared at

the sight of her babies, enchanted if confused. She absolutely could not be six months pregnant. She hadn't had a partner in over a year before Cody, and that was the only time she'd had sex since then. It was impossible, and she couldn't explain what she was looking at, but she decided not to argue with the doctor.

Perhaps she should get a second opinion, and she would definitely research any issues that might cause infants to grow faster than they should, but she was too tired and shocked to muster another response at the moment. "I must have miscalculated," she muttered, even though she knew it wasn't true.

---

*L*ess than an hour later, with two pictures in her purse of the babies in her womb, Jade made her way back into the university. She really wanted to go home and collapse in her own bed and sleep for twenty-four hours straight, but there were details to sort through before she could allow herself that luxury. Besides, in her current state, she wasn't certain she could sleep anyway.

It kept running through her mind that she was six months pregnant, which made no sense. She just couldn't accept the number the doctor had given her. It defied all logic and reason. She was certain it hadn't been an immaculate conception, but she had no other explanation for how she could be farther along than she thought. She was certain she hadn't been two months pregnant when she was with Cody, so what was going on?

She drew to a halt as she entered her office, a small cry escaping her. Where she had left order, now chaos reigned. The bookshelves had been tipped over, papers were scattered on the floor, and someone had upended the drawers of her desk. She shook her head, struggling to grasp the latest development. Who would break into her office, and why?

She stepped into the office, intent on calling security, but froze when a voice from the doorway sent a shiver down her spine.

"I love what you've done with the place." The words were neutral, but the voice was clearly angry. It also sent chills of want down her spine, and she turned around to face Cody, uncertain how he'd found her, and not sure if she was happy to see him. Her libido said yes, but her mind was conflicted.

She was even more conflicted when she got a good view of him. Gone were the jeans and leather, replaced by khakis and a sports coat. His long hair had been trimmed, and he was clean-shaven. Recalling how delicious that scruff felt rubbing against her body, she experienced a pang of remorse that he had shaved it off. She cleared her throat. "What are you doing here?"

He stepped into the office without invitation, moving closer to her as he closed the door behind him. "I've been waiting for you to get back."

She licked her lips, wondering when he would look down and see her stomach. When she took off her light cardigan, he wouldn't be able to miss the way the dress stretched tautly over her belly. "Why were you waiting for me?"

"Because you sneaked out of my bed after a fabulous night together without a word of parting. You never bothered to tell me you were going to be gone for months, and then you just disappeared. I figured we had things to talk about, so I've been checking your office periodically to see when you came back."

Her brain was awhirl, and she focused on an inconsequential detail to compensate. "Hasn't that made anyone suspicious, I mean, you hanging around my office?

He chuckled. "No, since mine is on the floor above yours, and I have to go by this way every day to exit the building anyway."

That was a surprise. "You work here?"

Cody seemed to take pleasure in her surprise. "I do. I'm Cody Lassiter, professor of zoology, and I hope to get tenure this year."

Her eyes widened surprise, and she was vaguely embarrassed to realize she had written him off as nothing more than a biker guy in a bar. It was the sort of response her parents would have had, and she was ashamed by that. "I see. You never said anything that night."

"We didn't do a lot of talking. That's why I'm willing to move past the fact that you just disappeared for four months without warning me that you'd be gone."

Her eyes widened. "I'm not in the habit of divulging personal details like that to someone I barely know."

He arched a brow. "But you sleep with them?"

She glared at him. "Now isn't a good time. Someone has ransacked my office, and I really don't have the energy to deal with a pointless dissection of our night together. I'd appreciate it if you would leave for now. We can set up an appointment later in the week."

His eyes flashed, and he scowled at her. "Someone ransacked your office?"

She waved a hand around. "Surely you don't think I leave it like this all the time?"

He shrugged, sounding bitter when he said, "I don't know. I haven't had a chance to get to know you well enough to say for sure."

"Well, I don't," she snapped, at the end of her patience. "When I left to go to the doctor, everything was perfect, and now it's a huge mess. I need to call security."

He paled, looking lightheaded for a moment as he swayed

before striding across the room toward her. She let out a yelp of surprise when he took her wrist in his hand. "What are you doing?"

"The doctor? Are you ill?"

As though the babies sensed her turbulence, they picked that moment to kick her. At least one did. She winced, more from guilt at the reminder of the discussion they really needed to have than any pain from the kick. "I'm okay, but I do need to talk to you about something."

He surprised her by sweeping her into his arms, hugging her as he let out an unsteady breath, as though overwhelmed by relief. A moment later, he stiffened and jerked back. His eyes were wide, and his expression was grim when he looked down at her stomach. "You're pregnant."

She nodded, bracing herself for angry words, unfounded accusations, or perhaps for him to simply turn around and walk away.

Instead, he surprised her by leaning down and pressing his face against her stomach. She yelped in surprise, but it was over almost as soon as it had begun, and he stood up fully again. "Why didn't you tell me?"

She blinked. "I just got back from Africa. I've barely had time to do anything besides catalog our finds and see the doctor."

"I see." He crossed his arms over his chest as he took a step back. "Were you planning to tell me at some point?"

She nodded. "I wasn't sure if I could find you again, but I had planned to visit the bar this evening and talk to your nephew, hoping he could give me a lead. I thought you were part of a biker gang or something, so I didn't know if I'd be able to find you."

A sinking sensation filled her as she realized he was not going to take it nearly as well when she divulged how far along the doctor estimated she was. She knew it was impossible, but Cody barely knew her. He was unlikely to believe she hadn't had a lover two months before him, and he would probably doubt paternity. Since they'd used a condom, she was surprised he hadn't insisted on a DNA test right away.

The cowardly part of her wanted to put off the revelation, and she decided to embrace that, just for a short time. When she was better rested and could meet with Cody again, then she would show him the pictures and tell him what the doctor had said, while maintaining the truth.

That was all she could do, though she was certain it would eventually denigrate into an argument, with name-calling slung in her direction, and ultimately require a DNA test and a court order for custody and child support arrangements.

She dreaded the whole idea, so she didn't fight when Cody took her into his arms again, rubbing her lower back as though he sensed instinctively which spot was already starting to cause her pain. She moaned with pleasure as he pressed his fingers into her lumbar area, massaging gently. "Oh, that feels good."

He laughed softly. "I've missed the sounds you make when I'm touching you, Jade."

She blinked in surprise at the revelation. If he was telling her the truth, that meant he'd thought about her while she was gone. She'd certainly thought about him multiple times, even before realizing they had accidentally created a life together.

Two lives, she hastily amended. At the time, she hadn't known that though, and she had logically assumed she was carrying one baby, not two, and she'd been unable to stop thinking about Cody, particularly in the moments where she wasn't occupied with anything else, though they were few and far between.

At night, she had lain in her narrow camping cot and

wished she was back in that larger hotel bed with Cody. To find out he had thought of her during that time too was surprising, flattering, and maybe a little alarming. It indicated that perhaps she was more than a one-night stand to him. That was a daunting prospect, especially under the circumstances.

He stepped back, looking regretful. "Why don't you call security and report the break-in, and then I'll take you to dinner? After that, we can have talk."

It was a sound plan, but she couldn't deny she was nervous about the forthcoming conversation. She did as he suggested and contacted security, unsurprised when he waited beside her until the guards had come. She gave the report to the older one, though the younger one was the one taking notes. After taking her report, and assuring her someone from housekeeping would be in to help right the mess, the guards left.

She decided to be irresponsible and leave the wreckage for the time being. All of the items had been catalogued except for some smaller finds that were still stacked in the corner.

The crates had been disrupted, and she hoped nothing had been shattered, but a lot of it was already shards of pottery and sundries that weren't nearly as important or unusual as a couple of other items they had discovered. Those items were already with experts being evaluated and carbon dated.

There was nothing that couldn't wait until morning, and though she was dreading the conversation, she was happy to leave the scattered mess in her office as she walked out beside Cody a few minutes later. When he took her hand, it felt natural and right to hold it as they walked together.

It was only back in his proximity that she realized just

how badly she had missed the man with whom she had what was supposed to be a one-night stand. Her conviction that it had been just sex was shaky at best.

3

*C*ody's bear was grumpy to be sitting across the table from Jade. Cody was grumpy himself, though he was pleased to be back in her presence. The last four months without her had been sheer torture.

As soon as he'd smelled her across the bar, he'd known she was his mate, and though he hadn't wanted to rush her, now he wished he had revealed everything to her that first night and bitten her to claim her as his mate. If he'd had any clue she was going to be departing for four months, he certainly would have done so and found a way to rearrange his schedule last-minute to accompany her wherever she went.

She'd mentioned something about Africa, and he made a mental note to ask her about it later, but right now, his attention was split between his bear's desire for her, which he shared, and his shock that he was going to be a father.

Elation filled him as she opened her purse to hand him the sonographic pictures. He looked down at the images, having already been warned there were two of them. The twins looked beautiful to his untrained eyes, and he could make out definite features. They looked like babies rather than little blobs. His insides softened, and his bear purred his satisfaction at the realization that his mate carried his cubs.

It also added new pressure to the relationship. He'd planned to give her time and move slowly once she returned. That plan had gone out the window in light of the knowledge she was pregnant with his babies.

He was going to claim her. And he was going to do it as soon as possible.

He just hoped he could gain her cooperation with the minimal amount of fuss. He couldn't in good conscience give her the mating bite until she consented. That was a taboo thing in their culture, and only the lowest of scumbags would do such a thing.

He grinned at her. "They look beautiful. Do you know the gender?"

Her eyes widened, and she laughed. "I never even thought to ask Dr. Grayson. I guess I was still just shocked myself."

He arched a brow. "You were surprised to find out you're pregnant?" He cast a doubtful glance at her stomach, which was beautifully rounded, making his fingers itch to touch it. Her breasts had also grown larger, and he and his bear both purred at the idea of exploring the new contours. His cock was hard and aching for her, but her visible concern quickly cut through his desire. "What's wrong?"

She shrugged. "I wasn't surprised to learn I'm pregnant, but the doctor did tell me something that was…irregular."

His heart stuttered for a moment. "Is there something wrong with the babies?"

She shrugged, looking uncertain. "The doctor said they're healthy, but she also said…" She trailed off, biting her lip as though bracing herself for something unpleasant.

"Said what?" he prompted gruffly. "I need to know if there's a problem with the cu—babies."

"She didn't have an explanation for me, but I didn't probe as much as I should have. I was still in shock. I'm afraid they might have something like gigantism."

He blinked. "What?"

She shrugged. "It's just a theory that popped into my head. It would explain why they appear to be bigger than they should."

Relief swept through him as he realized the problem. "How far along did the doctor guess you are?"

"She said six months." The way her mouth tightened indicated she was preparing herself for a blowup. Clearly, his mate expected him to attack her, accuse her of vile things, and storm out of the restaurant.

Instead, Cody leaned across the table and took her hand in his. "There's a perfectly valid explanation for that, but it's not something I can tell you in public. Let's have dinner, and then we'll go back to your place or mine for a more in-depth conversation."

After a moment, she nodded, and there was a hint of relief in her eyes. He hoped it was because he had eased her concerns over the twins, and not because she was relieved that he hadn't blown up at her. He didn't like the idea of her expecting him to be mean or angry. All he wanted to do was take care of her, though he knew he had to convince her of the strength of their connection first. It was going to be a challenge to claim his mate, but he was up for it.

He'd do anything to keep Jade. And his babies.

4

_____

*C*ody lived a few streets over from her, still within easy walking distance of the university. His place was closer to the restaurant where they had eaten, so she had acquiesced to the suggestion they go to his place.

It was a neat and orderly apartment, though a bit impersonal. There was a shelf full of an eclectic assortment of books, and a couple of picture frames on the wall with Cody and an older couple, but nothing else that gave a personal touch to the apartment.

The walls were still white, and he hadn't even added any throw rugs to the hardwood floor. His furniture was new, but mismatched. It was clearly a bachelor's pad, but at least it didn't have the requisite revolving door and drop-down bed. She couldn't help picturing Quagmire's set up from "Family Guy," and she was happy to realize the idea didn't gel at all with what she knew of Cody.

Admittedly, that wasn't much, but she was optimistic that would change. He clearly wanted more than the one night they'd had together, and he hadn't freaked out about the pregnancy. He hadn't shied away or accused her of being a whore when she'd divulged how far along the doctor thought the babies were. Instead, he claimed to have an explanation.

That alone would have gotten her back to his apartment, but she couldn't deny her rampant libido was hoping for a different outcome entirely. It had been four months, but it felt like forty years since they had been together.

She wasn't accustomed to sleeping around, but of the few affairs she'd had, she couldn't recall ever craving a man this intensely before, and she'd certainly never pined for one while she was parted from him for months on end. To have such a connection with a man whom she barely knew was strange, but also kind of wonderful.

She sat down on the brown leather sofa, and he took the seat beside her, though he didn't infringe on her personal space.

Dammit.

Perhaps it was for the best, because she needed to focus on the babies for the moment before allowing any carnal thoughts to interrupt. "You didn't seem all that shaken by the news that the babies are larger than they should be."

He shook his head. "That's because they aren't. My people have shorter gestation periods. Six months versus nine for humans."

Her heart seized for a moment, and fear filled her at his words. Great, he was clearly unhinged. She licked her dry lips, trying to proceed cautiously as she began to work out a plan to make it to the front door. "Oh. That's interesting."

He shot her a pissy look. "I'm not a nut job, and you don't have to patronize me."

She shook her head. "I wasn't. I'm fascinated to hear all about your...people. You aren't human then?" She felt like an idiot for having the conversation, but it seemed safer to play along until she had an opening to escape.

Crushing disappointment was trying to take over as she

realized all the half-spun dreams she'd been indulging in over the last few hours were coming to a screeching halt. No matter how attractive she found Cody, she couldn't continue the relationship, or whatever it was, with him being a possible danger to her and the children.

He rolled his eyes. "Do try to keep an open mind. Since you're a professor, with a specialty in archaeology, you should be capable of that."

It was her turn to roll her eyes. "My mind is perfectly open, and I'm waiting with bated breath to hear your theory."

"It's simple enough really. I'm a bear-shifter."

She stared at him in disbelief, finding it was worse than she'd thought. She had braced herself to hear something like he thought he was an alien, but this seemed even more dire. "What is a bear-shifter?"

"I can turn into a bear."

5

*Y*ep, it was definitely worse than she had expected.

"That's fascinating," she mocked. "Were you cursed? Was it a magical spell?"

He let out a snort. "Don't be a smartass. You might think you're being subtle, but it's clear as day that you think I'm crazy."

Though she wanted to placate him, her temper was starting to fray. "I imagine you get that reaction a lot when you share your secret."

He surprised her by laughing. "I've never told anyone outside of my family. We don't go bandying it about to everyone we meet."

Her eyes widened. "Your family is in on it...shares this belief?"

He let out a long sigh, clearly exasperated. "It's not anything mystical or magical. *Ursa sapiens* simply followed a different evolutionary path from *homo sapiens*. I have a human form and a bear form. If you're done being skeptical, I'll prove it to you."

She braced herself. "Of course. Please do so." She had no

idea what to expect, but she guessed he was going to don a bearskin rug or something and dance around pretending to be half-man and half-animal.

The sad thing was, he probably wasn't pretending. He very likely believed his own delusion, and she rubbed her stomach in a consoling fashion, as though comforting the babies over the fact their father was a complete loon.

He stood up and started to undress. Panicked, she put up her hand. "That is not happening tonight."

He laughed. "Relax. I just don't want to rip my clothes."

She nodded, feeling surreal when she said, "I'm sure it must be expensive to replace your wardrobe when you're a bear-shifter."

He rolled his eyes. "We usually shift when we're naked, Jade."

She sat as quietly as possible, though her gaze continuously darted to the door. She hoped when he was in the process of his elaborate costume change that she would have an opening to run for it.

After that, she wasn't certain what she was going to do, but if he continued to pester her, she'd have to get a restraining order and probably turn him over to the authorities so he could get the mental help he needed.

She was so busy thinking about her escape route that it took her a moment to realize Cody's form had changed. There was no bearskin rug or elaborate costume. Where he'd been, now stood an impressive brown bear, and it appeared to be grinning at her. It had sparkling white teeth, which would be strange in a bear, unless he had access to whitening toothpaste and an electronic toothbrush.

She looked at the bear, opening her mouth to scream in fear, when she realized it had the same blue eyes as Cody. She let out a little *yeep* of fright instead, her rational brain trying to find an explanation even as her primal brain embraced it, along with a surge of fear.

She was instantly thrown back to the days when humans were prey, and her fight-or-flight response kicked in. She scrambled up from the couch and rushed across the room, running as fast as she could as she heard the bear's claws click behind her.

She threw open the door and plunged down the hallway, not even stopping for a second when she heard Cody calling out her name. She didn't know if he had spoken in his bear form, or if he had transformed back. She didn't want to know. It was too much to deal with, so she ran. Escape was the only thing on her mind.

He caught up with her less than a block from his apartment, his large hand on her upper arm forcing her to arrest her flight. She stopped as she pulled free of him, upsetting her center of gravity and almost falling. If it hadn't been for his steadying hands on her hips, she would have collided with the sidewalk.

The realization was enough to bring her to her senses, though she remained wary. She couldn't risk injuring her baby just because she was trying to escape its father. Babies, she reminded herself.

"I'm not going to hurt you."

She hugged herself defensively. "How do I know that? I don't know you at all, Cody."

"We'll fill in the details with time, but you need to know you can trust me. I would never hurt you or our children."

Looking into his blue eyes, she could see only sincerity, but she was still frightened. "I'm going home now."

His lips tightened, but he didn't try to argue. "I'll walk you there."

She shook her head. "No, thank you." She needed to

escape him, to have time to think and sort through everything she'd seen.

He crossed his arms over his chest, looking stern. "I insist. You're pregnant, and you don't need to be wandering the streets after dark alone. You're a vulnerable target."

Jade wanted to continue arguing, but she realized he was right. They were in a fairly safe neighborhood, but anything could happen to anyone at any time. After all, she had just seen the most fantastical thing in her life, and clearly Cody expected her to absorb it easily.

Maybe she was being unfair to him, since he hadn't tried to force her back to his place. She was in no frame of mind to be completely fair at the moment, though. She was still in a state of shock.

Questions crowded her brain as she walked beside him, maintaining a subtle distance between them. She froze in her tracks when a disturbing thought came to her. "Are the babies going to be like you?"

He stopped along with her. "Yes, I'm sure they will be. The gene that allows shifting is a dominant trait, though there has been occasional offspring between human and bear-shifters that couldn't shift. It's unlikely, though."

She grimaced. "Are they going to look like bears when they come out?" She couldn't get past that thought. If that were the case, she was going to have to be knocked out so they could be born, and good luck explaining that to Dr. Grayson. Her face paled, and she swayed unsteadily. "How am I ever going to explain this to my doctor? She's going to know I'm farther along than I should be next time I go in."

He put a hand on her shoulder, which had the dual effect of soothing her while also reminding her that those hands could transform into paws with vicious claws at a moment's notice. She shivered, not entirely certain if it was from fear or the pleasant sensation of having his hand on her shoulder.

She was a completely jumbled mess around him, and she needed time to sort out how she felt.

"To answer your first question, no. They might have some excess hair for a couple of days, but it'll fall out soon enough. They'll have some different nutritional needs from a typical human baby, but they won't be able to shift until puberty."

A wave of relief swept through her. That was one less thing to worry about. "Will they grow faster too, since the pregnancy is accelerated?"

"A bit faster, probably. They'll probably gain milestones more quickly too, but it won't be anything too out of place that will make anyone comment on them being far older or more advanced than they should be."

She let out an uneven sigh. "That's good to know. I guess I have roughly thirteen years to come to grips with the reality that my babies will be able to shift into bears."

Thirteen years didn't sound nearly long enough, but she was aided by the fact that she already loved the twins fiercely. She could probably accept Cody's shifter side too if she loved him. She didn't, of course. It had only been one night, and she barely knew him, but she was certain if love was there, it would help ease her doubts.

"For your second question, we have contacts, and some of our people are in different professions, especially here in Seattle. I know of at least two obstetricians who won't bat an eye at taking on a new patient whose pregnancy is accelerated."

She was intrigued by the idea, though she really liked Dr. Grayson. "I'll give it some thought." Realizing they were still standing in the middle of the sidewalk, she started walking again.

Questions still zoomed through her mind, but she felt more at peace than she had a few minutes ago after being reassured of the worst details weighing on her mind weren't as dire as she had assumed. "I'm sorry if I offended you by running out, but this is a lot to take in."

He nodded. "I'm aware of that, and I'm trying not to take it personally that you ran away from me and don't want me to touch you." His tone was cool, but there was a hint of hurt underlying it.

She winced, feeling embarrassed, but unable to conquer her need to maintain a barrier between them. They crossed the last two blocks in silence, and it was the awkward kind that made her eager to escape. When they reached her apartment building, she tried to leave him in the lobby. "Thank you for walking me home."

"I'll walk you to your door. I want to make sure you get there safely."

She let out a sigh of impatience, but decided it would be easier just to let him follow behind her than argue about it. Her back was hurting, probably from her impromptu run, and she just wanted to take a warm bath and relax. If possible, she'd like to shut off her brain for a while.

But now that she knew the father of her children was also a bear? Any chance of relaxation seemed unlikely.

6

*A*fter her bath, she needed at least twelve hours of uninterrupted sleep to make up for the poor rest she'd gotten over the last few months. She loved being an archaeologist, but that often included living in rough conditions, which had never been her favorite thing. Her idea of vacation was a five-star resort, not pitching a tent in the middle of nowhere.

She was conscious of him walking directly behind her, his chest brushing against her back with every step. It was an innocuous touch, but it was enough to send her heart racing and shift her hormones into overdrive. It was an abrupt reminder that she still found him as attractive as she had before, even though she knew more about him now, including what she presumed was his darkest secret.

Not that he seemed ashamed by it, and nor should he. If he was telling her the truth, and she had little reason to doubt that, it was simply an evolutionary difference between his people and hers. When she regarded it with a purely logical bent, it made her curious to know more. It was only when she allowed her emotions to filter in that panic tried to return.

When they reached the door, she drew her line in the sand. She opened the door and then turned to face him, blocking his ability to enter. "Thank you for walking me home."

His lips twitched. "You already said that..." He trailed off, his eyes widening before a grim expression took over. "Step away from the doorway."

She crossed her arms over her chest and glared at him. "This is my home, and I'm staying here. Without you. It's time for you to leave."

With an impatient sigh, he clamped a hand on her shoulder and dragged her physically from the doorway, ignoring her squawk of outrage. "Turn around and look at your apartment."

She did so, letting out a horrified gasp when she saw the mess strewn about her living room. Someone had broken into her apartment, and it was an even worse mess than her office had been earlier. She was shocked by what she witnessed, and completely unable to figure out why someone would break into her office and her apartment. Was it a random coincidence?

That seemed unlikely.

Abruptly, she realized Cody was on the phone, and she tried to focus on his conversation as she stared at the debris that had once been her cozy little apartment décor.

She felt violated, and anger was stronger than fear in that moment. If the person who had done that was still in her apartment, she imagined she could take them down single-handedly with her current level of rage, pregnant or not.

Of course she had better sense than that, and she backed away from the apartment when she realized the vandal could still be inside. She focused on Cody's conversation, quickly realizing he was reporting the incident to the police after asking for a specific detective. When he had hung up, she asked, "Is that Strand guy one of yours?"

He shook his head. "He's a wolf-shifter, but we're friends, and he can be discreet. Not that I have any reason to think this is linked to the shifter community. No one knows yet that you're my mate, and I don't have any enemies of which I'm aware."

She froze, dismayed at the warm glow of pleasure sweeping through her in a discordant mess. "I'm your what?"

He stilled, his cheeks darkening a bit with a flush. "I shouldn't have said that this soon."

"What does that mean? I'm your mate? In your world, if you screw someone, have you mated?"

He grimaced. "Of course not. Bears mate for life—at least bear-shifters do. We have good instincts. When I smelled my mate—you—I could tell by your scent that you belong to us. It's the same for female bear-shifters, of course. When I smelled you across the bar, my bear knew right away you were ours."

Her laugh held a definite note of hysteria she couldn't repress. "That's a special talent to have. What if your mate doesn't want to be your mate?"

He sagged against the wall, looking temporarily defeated. "Then I guess I'm going to live the rest of my life in misery, alone. I hope you'll change your mind after you get over the shock and at least give me a chance. All I'm asking is for you to get to know me, and let me be part of our children's life. I want you as mine, but I'm never going to force you to do anything you don't want to."

Before she could formulate a reply, a man in his late thirties came up the stairs. He wore jeans and a polo shirt, but there was something about him that screamed "police."

It was funny, because Jade certainly didn't have a built-in

law enforcement detector. She'd never even gotten a ticket, and she had no reason to be fearful of the police, or to identify them when they were undercover. She just knew this was the detective by the way he carried himself. As he got closer, the visible bulge of a hip holster also reinforced her assumption.

Cody greeted the newcomer with a handshake before turning to put his arm around Jade and draw her closer. She didn't miss the fact that he didn't drop his arm once he brought her to face the detective, and nor did it escape her attention that she didn't step away or shrug him off. It felt good to have him touching her and offering some comfort and support, though she was conflicted by feeling that way.

"Detective Jason Strand, this is Dr. Jade Barnes. It was her apartment that's been burgled."

"I don't actually know if anything was stolen, but they've torn everything to shreds." She was saddened by the loss of her things and angered by the fact someone had broken into her private sanctuary to destroy it.

The detective shook her hand before he pulled out his gun. "I imagine they're gone by now, but you two wait out here while I double-check." A second later, he slipped inside the apartment, carefully closing the door behind himself. Presumably, he wanted to block any person trying to flee, or at least slow their escape time.

Jade leaned against the wall, awkwardly trying to rub her back as she did so. She didn't object when Cody gently turned her to face the wall, urging her to extend her back by tugging lightly on her hips. It was uncanny how well she understood exactly what he wanted from her without a word spoken between them.

It should have been more alarming than it was, and she realized the reality of it all was starting to sink in. The terror and irrational fear she had experienced earlier were starting to fade, though she wasn't quite at the point of acceptance just yet.

His fingers were getting her closer though, she had to concede, as he began to rub her lower back. He instinctively found the spot that was bothering her the most, and she moaned low in her throat. "I could get used to this."

There was a trace of amusement in his tone. "I'll be happy to rub you whenever you'd like. All you have to do is ask."

That would require accepting his revelations and agreeing to spend more time with him. It would also require a small measure of pride sacrificed to the altar of humility to request anything from him.

She was used to being independent and doing things on her own, but asking for a back rub from the man who had impregnated her didn't seem like something that would rob her of her feminine power.

She gave a reluctant nod and let herself melt into the blissful feeling of his hands on her body.

7

The pain had eased considerably just from a short massage by the time the detective returned to them. His gun was back in his holster, and he was alone, indicating no one had been in the apartment. He opened the door wide and gestured for them to enter. "Come in and do an inventory please, Dr. Barnes. I need to know if anything is missing."

At first, she wandered aimlessly through the apartment, feeling lost and out of sorts. It was like a foreign place to her now, and the warm and comforting vibe that she always got from stepping inside the door was gone.

Her trust in the place was shattered, and she knew she couldn't sleep there tonight. She might never be able to again, which enraged her. The building was close to the university, meaning she could walk to work, and she had liked the quiet and coziness. Someone had robbed that from her, and a surge of rage filled her.

She struggled to calm down and focus on determining if anything was missing. The television and her laptop were exactly where she had left them this morning, as was an expensive stereo system. This clearly hadn't been a run-of-the-mill burglary, because nothing of any value appeared to be missing.

She wandered from the living room to the kitchen, eyeing it quickly. Whoever had broken into her apartment had clearly done a less thorough examination of the kitchen, because it wasn't quite the mess that the living room was. Her stand mixer and countertop convection oven were still there, and they were the only expensive appliances that might have interested a burglar, though she doubted they would have.

Moving on, she peeked into the bathroom, which was mostly undisturbed, though someone had left up the toilet seat. "It looks like it was a guy who broke in."

The detective had shadowed her, and he asked now, "What makes you think that?"

She waved to the toilet seat. "He left the lid and the seat up. It's not something I would do. Trust me."

He made a note of it, looking slightly amused. She continued down the hallway, pausing at the room she used as an office. It was a complete and total mess, even worse than the devastation at her university office. Papers were strewn about, and the desktop computer she kept there was completely gone, though they had left the monitor. Whoever had broken in was definitely looking for something, though she wasn't sure what.

She moved gingerly through the mess on the office floor, heading for her filing cabinet. It was open, and she had left it closed. She wasn't surprised that it was open, since there were papers everywhere, but she was curious to see if she could determine which files had been of interest.

It was difficult to tell, since everything was such a mess, and she let out a sigh as she moved on. Feeling dejected, she sank into her computer chair and stared around her at the debris. "I don't think anything is missing besides my desktop, and I'm not sure why they'd want that, but would leave the laptop. It makes no sense."

"Perhaps they assumed all your work-related things were done on your desktop. Or maybe they searched through your laptop already and decided there was nothing of interest," suggested Cody.

The detective offered his own theory. "Maybe they cloned your hard drive on the laptop, but couldn't manage to do so with the desktop, so they were forced to take it."

She grimaced. "They can do that?"

Strand nodded grimly. "If they know what they're doing, they can. I'd suggest calling your bank and having all your cards and accounts changed or closed down in case the person got your sensitive financial information."

She let out a low groan of disgust. "That's going to be terribly inconvenient." Not that she was going to ignore the detective's advice, because she didn't want whomever had broken in to rob her blind. Somehow, she thought this was about something other than money though, but why take the chance?

As she stood up, her hand brushed against the drawer of her desk, and she looked down when she realized it was closed, but not completely. She had locked it earlier, and she tugged it open. It stuck for a moment, but whoever had been in her office had broken the lock, and it finally yielded. The drawer was now empty. "They took something."

"What's that?" asked Detective Strand as Cody came to stand behind her, putting a comforting hand on her shoulder.

"I just got back from a dig at a Sumerian outpost. At least that's what we surmise it is, though we're still waiting for carbon dating and confirmation in other ways. All my notes and pictures from the dig are gone."

The detective seemed surprised. "You think someone broke in to steal your academic records?"

She shrugged. "It makes sense. Someone also broke into my office at the university earlier in the day."

The detective looked troubled. "Why didn't you say something about that sooner?"

She lifted her shoulder. "I guess I just didn't think about it. We reported it to the school security officers, but it will be handled internally, and I didn't make the connection. I was still in shock about learning..." She trailed off, looking over her shoulder and upward at Cody uncertainly. "About things."

The detective looked at them both for a moment before nodding, apparently realizing to what she referred. "Well, I'll file a report, and someone from the CSI unit will come out to dust for fingerprints and look for forensic evidence. In the meantime, you can't stay here."

"I don't want to anyway. I'm not sure I can ever sleep here again and feel safe."

The detective reached into his pocket and pulled out a business card. "You can reach me here if you think of anything else, and I'll be in touch if I learn anything. Where will you be staying?"

"The Hilton by the university," said Jade.

At the same time, Cody said, "She'll be with me."

The detective arched a brow, looking mildly amused. "I'll let you two sort that out, but at least I have a vague idea how to find you."

A few moments later, he left them, and she went to her bedroom to pack a case. Cody followed behind her, but she didn't look at him or talk to him. He was being a presumptuous ass, and he was in for a rude awakening.

She definitely wasn't staying with him.

8

A couple of hours later, she stared at her reflection in the mirror in the bathroom attached to his bedroom, still not entirely sure how she'd ended up yielding to his demand that she stay with him. She knew it had something to do with his logical arguments, combined with the naked need in his eyes. She had a feeling she'd lost the battle when he had implored her to let him keep her and the babies safe, sensing he needed to have that role. Plus, her own heart was guiding her to this path, despite her brain's stubborn resistance.

Delaying the inevitable could be put off no longer, so she slipped out of his bathroom and into his bedroom, staring at him warily. "I still think I should sleep on the couch."

He shook his head, his jaw firmed. "You're not sleeping on the couch. It's lumpy and uncomfortable, and you already have a backache. Besides, don't pregnant women need like ten pillows?"

"Two or three," she conceded. She arched her brow as she saw him walk to the bed and pull back the sheets and blanket. "Turndown service even, huh?"

He laughed, though his heart didn't appear to be in an amused place. "Yeah, this is better than the Hilton."

She approached the bed and slid in, deliberately picking the side he hadn't folded back for her, though she couldn't say why. A moment later, she almost bounced out of bed as she scrambled to get up when he laid down beside her. "What are you doing?"

He gave her a look as though she were mentally deficient. "I'm going to bed. What does it look like?"

She glared at him. "It looks like I'm sleeping on the couch then."

He groaned. "No one is sleeping on that uncomfortable thing. Just go to sleep."

She started to scramble out of bed, which was more difficult than it should be due to her expanding stomach and slightly clumsy moves these days. She let out a cry of protest when he put his arm around her waist, gently pulling her back against him before clamping her against the heat of his body. "Let me go."

"Calm down and go to sleep, Jade." He sounded exhausted, and she certainly was. "You know I'm not going to hurt you, and I promise I won't touch you in any inappropriate ways until you're asking me to. Just go to sleep for tonight. You and the babies both need your rest."

She felt like she should keep protesting, but it was obscenely comfortable in his bed, and she moaned softly when her body sank into the memory foam. It wasn't unpleasant having his arm around her or his body pressed so close to her own. She decided she was too tired to keep fighting, at least for the moment, and surrendered to sleep before her head was on the pillow.

---

*S*ometime in the night, she had rolled over to face him, and she woke with her face pressed against his chest. His hair tickled her nose, and she pulled back slightly, which instinctively caused him to tighten his arms around her. She held her breath for a moment, wondering if he would awaken, and she wriggled slightly, more in an experimental fashion than an actual desire to escape.

It felt too good being held in his arms, and she knew she was going to have a difficult time tearing herself away. With some perspective and space, the revelation he'd given her last night didn't seem quite as shocking or terrifying. It was difficult to worry about the fact that he could change his form when the form he held against her was so perfect and awe-inspiring. And panty-melting, she conceded with a twitch of her lips.

"Good morning," he said, his chest rumbling and sending vibrations through her body.

She looked up at him, startled when his eyes went from closed to fully open, appearing alert, in a millisecond. "You're awake?" she asked, though it was a stupid question.

His lips twitched. "I've been awake off and on throughout the night. I was worried about you, and having you sleep so close made it difficult to fall asleep."

She frowned in concern. "It's a king-size bed, so there should have been plenty of room for both of us. I'm sorry if I kept you awake though."

He flashed her a lazy grin as he cupped her buttocks and pressed her pelvis gently against his to show her the strength of his arousal. "That was what kept me awake most of the night off and on, Jade. It's definitely your fault, so you should feel terrible about it."

She rolled her eyes at his teasing tone. "It's not my fault you can't control yourself."

His voice lowered an octave, turning smoky with desire. "I don't think I can control myself, at least that reaction, around you. When we're ninety years old, I'll still be getting a hard-on every night just from sleeping with you in my arms."

She wanted to call him on his presumption, even as she wanted to cling to him and start planning their future. Neither option was viable, because her screaming bladder reminded her why she had woken to start with. "I have to use the restroom."

He nodded, releasing his hold on her so she could roll away. "I'll start breakfast."

"You cook too?"

He nodded, pausing for a moment before leaving the bed. "I cook well. What else do I do well?"

She could have listed a few things for him, but his ego was already as large as his... She shut down that thought and forced a prim expression. "I'm not sure what else you do well, but I hope you really are a good cook. I'm starving."

"Any requests?"

She shook her head as she pushed through the bathroom door, closing it behind her. It was a relief to escape the wicked temptation in his eyes and the smoky drawl of his voice. He was far too attractive to make it easy to sort out how she felt when she was so close to him.

Not that she thought distance would really do much to clarify her perspective. She had a feeling that even when she wasn't with him, she was going to be thinking about him on a disturbingly regular basis. And not simply because of his fantastical ability to transform into a bear at will. It was the man himself who preoccupied her thoughts, and she couldn't imagine that changing any time soon.

9

*C*ody focused on making a huge breakfast for Jade, uncertain how much she needed to eat. He knew a pregnant bear-shifter ate a prodigious amount of food, but he wasn't sure if it was the same with humans. Human women also had a tendency to get too concerned with their weight, though he didn't know if that affected pregnant women also.

He imagined they were more focused on being healthy and taking care of their babies, but he wasn't certain. Either way, the obsession with being stick-thin was puzzling to him. Jade's curves were one of the things he loved about her, and the way her softness molded to his hardness was a delicious sensation. He loved being able to grasp her fleshy hips and sink into her liquid heat while feeling like he wasn't going to break her.

The uncomfortable tightening of his pajama pants reminded him to focus on breakfast before he burned the bacon. It proved a difficult task, especially when her scent permeated the area. Having her sleep in his arms had left him marked by her scent, and it increased his urgency to do the same. It had been torture to wake with her in his arms and not make love to her, especially knowing he couldn't yet deliver the mating bite anyway. That would mark her as his and ward off all other male shifters who might show an interest, but it was too soon for that. She had to consent and understand she was agreeing to a lifetime commitment before he could bite her.

In the meantime, he'd have to content himself with taking care of her and the babies, which was no small task. He was still humbled and a little bit terrified by the idea that his mate would be having his cubs in approximately eight weeks. He'd barely had time to grow accustomed to the idea, and he was soon going to be a father. He was excited and impatient to meet them despite his slight anxiety.

First, he had to sort out what was happening with Jade and ensure she was safe. It seemed obvious someone was targeting her for a reason, but they'd have to go through one angry bear-shifter to get to her.

He looked up when he detected her scent growing nearer, smelling and hearing her before he saw her enter the kitchen. "Perfect timing. I was just finishing up the hash browns."

She took a seat at the table, and his cock twitched at her moan of pleasure when he placed a plate before her a moment later. It might have been in response to the food, but his brain conjured memories of their night together, when he'd heard that same sounds of pleasure as they had lost themselves in each other. "I hope you're hungry."

Her eyes widened as she looked down at her plate. "I'd better be. I think you made enough for three lumberjacks here."

"You are eating for three now."

She giggled. "I think that gives me like five hundred extra calories a day, not five thousand." Despite her teasing, she lifted her fork and dug into the homemade hash browns, crisp bacon, grilled tomatoes, and over-easy eggs. She must have doubted her ability to finish it, so she looked surprised when her plate was almost cleared a half-hour later.

She leaned back, rubbing her stomach as she groaned. "I can't believe I ate most of that. It was delicious, but there was so much of it."

A warm glow of pride filled him to know he'd taken care of her and met that need. He wanted to meet all her needs, and he hoped she would give him a chance to do so. "I'm glad you enjoyed it." He had mechanically eaten his own breakfast, too engrossed with watching her to really pay attention to what he was doing. Somehow, he'd managed to get all the food in his mouth without making a huge mess, and he was grateful for that.

He stood up and retrieved their plates, shooing her back to the table when she tried to rise to help him. "Just rest for a moment."

She rolled her eyes. "I just slept for ten hours, and I ate a huge breakfast. I haven't really exerted myself, so there's not much reason to rest."

"Other than the fact that you're growing two new little humans," he reminded her as he rinsed off the dishes before opening the dishwasher.

"Kind of human," she said with a hitch in her voice, her fear and uncertainty showing through.

The tone gutted him, but he forced his expression to remain neutral when he turned to look at her. "Our babies will be as human as you, but they'll just possess an extra talent. There's no reason to be afraid of them, or hold back and not bond. I guarantee you'll love our children whether they're in human form or bear form."

Her expression softened, though she looked vaguely guilty. "I know I will. I'm just a little nervous about everything. I didn't expect this. It was supposed to be just one night of sex."

He smiled ruefully. "Maybe for you, but I knew right away that you were my mate. I always planned this to be a forever event."

She looked torn on her response, and he took pity on her by flipping on the television on the counter and allowing her a distraction while he finished the dishes. Not every conversation could turn into a heartfelt plea for her to give him a chance.

The news came on, and he listened with half an ear as he finished cleaning the kitchen, freezing when he heard her gasp. He looked up at her, finding her attention glued to the screen, so he looked there as well. The perfectly coiffed blonde anchorwoman was wearing a suitable expression of sympathy as she recounted scant details of a professor who had been murdered in his office at the college. He froze, and his gaze darting back to her. "Did you know him?"

Slowly, she nodded. "Eli Deceric was the first professor I TA'd for. I got lucky and was hired at the university, so I didn't have to bounce all over the world to different ones in search of tenure. A big part of that was because of Dr. Deceric. He really liked me, and I liked him." Her expression turned troubled. "I also left a box of artifacts with him for carbon dating. He's one of the two experts at the university. I'd love to know if that box is still at the office, or if it's mysteriously disappeared."

"I'll give Jason a call."

Suddenly, she clapped a hand over her mouth, looking horrified. "We have to go to the college right now."

He frowned. "You're still in your pajamas, and I thought you might want to just take it easy today."

She shook her head, her urgency clear. "No, you don't understand. I left a box of artifacts from the dig site with Dr.

Deceric, but I also dropped off a rare and amazing find with Glenda Cross. She's the other expert at the university, and she's also the director of the Sumerian wing at the Burke Museum. She's an expert, and if someone is targeting items from the dig, and if they realize I left something with Glenda, they'll go after her next. We have to warn her and retrieve the artifact."

He wanted to insist that she rest, but her urgency was contagious. He knew she wouldn't rest if she was worried about her friend anyway, and he vaguely thought about suggesting he go check on her, but realized he didn't want to leave Jade alone. "Get dressed as quickly as you can then, and we'll find your friend."

*T*hey found Glenda Cross' office ransacked, with the old woman lying on the floor. Cody reached her first, though Jade was only a step or two behind. They knelt beside her, and she winced when she saw the blood matted in the professor's white hair. Feeling cowardly, she allowed Cody to be the one to check for a pulse, exhaling raggedly when he nodded to confirm he'd found one.

She retrieved her cell phone from her pocket and called nine-one-one before turning her attention back to Glenda. The old woman was unconscious, though her eyes fluttered occasionally, and Jade hoped that was a good sign, one indicating she would awaken soon.

"It seems someone's after something you brought her."

She nodded at Cody. "It must be the scepter of Inanna."

He looked confused. "The scepter of whom?"

"Inanna. She was the Sumerian goddess of fertility and love, among other roles." When she looked down, she saw Glenda's eyes had opened, though they appeared unfocused.

When the blue orbs collided with hers, she forced a reassuring smile. "Help will be here soon, Glenda. Just hold on."

"He..." She trailed off, and her eyes closed again. It was another minute or two before they opened again. "...Took...scepter."

She patted the professor on the shoulder. "It's okay. It's just an object. The most important thing is you're okay."

"Still...danger." Her eyes closed again, and this time they didn't reopen. It was a relief when the ambulance arrived less than five minutes later, with two brawny medics loading her onto a gurney and whisking her out of the room.

As they waited for campus security and the police to arrive, she looked around the mess and shivered slightly. "All this for an old artifact. Don't get me wrong. I'm an archaeologist, so I certainly appreciate the value of these finds, but not to the extent of destroying property and injuring an old lady."

He looked grim when he nodded. "And she said there's still danger. There's no way you can go back to your apartment."

Jade shook her head. "I wasn't planning to. I think I'm going to have to give it up. I don't think I'm in danger any longer, since the thief stole the scepter, but I don't think I can live there now. In the meantime, I can stay at my cousin's apartment while I look for a new place. She's off on a photojournalist assignment, so I doubt she'll mind."

He crossed his arms over his chest. "You'll stay with me."

She rolled her eyes. "There's no reason for that, but thank you." Her tone sounded less than grateful, but it was the best she could muster in the face of his bossiness.

Cody glared at her. "It's not safe for you to live alone right now."

She waved a hand. "Glenda's confused. She has a head injury, and she's older anyway. For all I know, she might have the beginning stages of dementia. Just because she thinks I'm in danger—and she didn't actually say I was specifically in danger—doesn't mean it's true."

He scowled at her. "It doesn't mean it isn't true either, but even if you aren't in danger from some thief, you're still carrying my children, and you're going to stay with me."

"And you're going to back the fuc—"

Someone clearing their throat at the doorway interrupted the vulgarity she had planned to say, and she flushed with embarrassment to have their argument overheard. She dropped the subject, embarrassed by the hint of amusement in the detective's face when she recognized Jason Strand in the doorway. A security officer from the university stood behind him, and she let out a sigh as she prepared herself for another round of questioning. It was the last thing she felt like dealing with, aside from arguing about living arrangements with Cody. She wasn't going to live with him, and that was final.

10

"*I* can't believe I'm back here again." She dropped her purse on the entryway table in his apartment and stared around for a moment, still not quite clear on how she'd ended up agreeing to come back to his place.

It had something to do with the deep, heartfelt conversation he'd promised he wanted to have with her, though she half-expected him to pull a Neanderthal routine and try to lock her in the apartment now that she was here. Still, a simple conversation couldn't hurt anything, and that was why she had yielded to his request to come back to his apartment—at least long enough to talk.

As she sat beside him on the couch, Jade realized the real challenge was keeping control of her rampant hormones when he was so close. His proximity made her heart race and her panties damp. She wanted to chalk it up to side effects of pregnancy, having heard the second trimester was notorious for increased libido, but it was an effect she only seemed to have around Cody.

She leaned back against the couch, trying to appear casual in her need to separate herself from him as much as possible.

She curled up into the corner, nonplussed when he remained seated beside her, taking her feet onto his lap instead of moving a cushion over. When he began to strip off her shoes, she frowned at him. "What are you doing?"

"Rubbing your feet."

That was a terrible idea. She opened her mouth to protest, but before she could decide if she really wanted to, he had stripped off her socks as well, and his thumbs began to glide over the underside of her feet. She let out a moan when he hit a spot that made her whole body relax, and she decided a foot massage wasn't going to deter her from leaving or convince her to stay when she didn't want to.

That was the crux of the matter though. She really did want to stay with him, but not because he was being noble and protecting her from a danger that didn't exist, or because she was carrying his children. He had spouted that information about her being his mate, but she just didn't see how it could work that way. "How did you really know I was your mate? Was that true?"

He looked offended, though he kept rubbing her feet. "Of course it was true. I haven't lied to you, and I never will. At least not deliberately."

She didn't know him as well as she should have, but as she looked at his expression before meeting his gaze, she was positive he was telling her the truth, at least about not lying to her. "But how can you know someone is meant to be your partner for life just by how they smell? It's crazy."

Cody shrugged. "It isn't crazy to me. It is what it is. Instinct runs deep in our kind, and we recognize our mates. I'm not sure what to say to convince you, but it's the truth. And the truth also is I want you to stay here with me, and I want to claim you as my mate."

She ran a hand through her hair, feeling frustrated and annoyed, though she couldn't say why. "We hardly know each other. We're talking about a lifelong relationship, and all we have between us is sex."

His eyes narrowed, and one of his hands moved from her foot to her belly, where he cupped the burgeoning mound gently. "And the children."

She let out a snort. "I'm not going to marry someone...er, mate with someone just because I'm pregnant. There has to be something more than that to make me change my mind, Cody."

"It's a lot more than just the babies, Jade. I recognized you as mine the moment I met you. You're probably looking for words of love, and I have no problem telling you that. I love you, and that's the truth. It's all wrapped up with instinct for me. I loved you before I met you, but now that I know you, I could never accept another mate. It's your right to reject me, and I'll have to accept it if you do, but I'll spend the rest of my life pining for you. I'm not trying to guilt you into anything. I'm simply telling you the truth. No other woman will do for me after I've been with you."

As far as lines went, it was a doozy, especially since it hit her right in the heart. In other circumstances, she would have suspected him of just spinning a line, or manipulating her for his own purposes, but he was just so sincere that it was difficult not to believe him. She let out a small sigh. "I can't say the same yet, Cody. I do like you, and I definitely feel something for you, but I can't label it as love. We hardly know each other."

He looked unhappy, but he didn't argue. "It's not the same for humans. This would have been easier if you'd been a bear-shifter too, but I'd rather have a difficult time with you than an easy time with someone else. All I'm asking for is for you to give me a chance and keep an open mind."

Her voice emerged as a smoky purr when she spoke again. "That's all you're asking for? Really? You don't think it's a good idea to have some trial runs on this mating thing, so I can decide with all the facts in mind?"

He arched a brow, looking intrigued. "Are you propositioning me, Dr. Barnes?"

She tilted her head to the side and giggled. "You know, Mr. Lassiter, I do believe I am." She had barely finished the sentence before he stood up and had her in his arms, striding to the bedroom. Perhaps it wasn't the smartest move, but it was the best one under the circumstances, and the only strategy she wanted to take.

She was more than happy to give Cody a chance to win her over to his point of view, even if it took a thousand nights in his bed to convince her. She was willing to do whatever it took. She giggled at the idea that sleeping with Cody would be a big sacrifice on her part as he laid her on the bed. It was no sacrifice at all to open her arms and welcome him into them a moment later.

She was a logical person, but with him in her arms, and emotions and hormones swaying her intellect, she found she could definitely get on board with the idea of instantly recognizing the person with whom you were meant to spend your life. Intellectually, it sounded ridiculous, but it appealed to the emotional side of her.

Cody stripped away the doctorate and all the years of training, reducing her once again to a woman with feminine instincts, and her instincts guided her to follow him to find her place with him. For once in her life, Jade surrendered to instinct over intellect, and she had no regrets.

11

The week flew by before she had realized it, and she was growing more certain every day that Cody was right about them being mates. When she wasn't teaching or at the university, she was with him. The time they spent together was usually relaxing, and the nights in his bed were the most passionate ones of her life.

The tantalizing idea of having this future spread before her for the rest of her life was definitely swaying her toward his request to allow him to claim her as his mate.

He'd explained the process, and she knew it involved him biting her to leave his scent, and to warn away other male bear-shifters. It was highly primitive and reminiscent of many of the antiquated marriage rituals performed throughout history. If she agreed to it, she was also going to insist on a more traditional human marriage, too.

They had plenty of time though, since she felt no need to be married before the children were born. It was better to be certain this was the future they both wanted than to rush into something that would end up causing them more hurt and disappointment in the future.

Not that she could imagine Cody actually hurting her. He went out of his way to be protective and loving, and though sometimes he was overly protective and kind of bossy, she usually gritted her teeth and reminded him politely to back off, knowing it came from a place of love. They were still working out the kinks and getting a feel for each other, but she was optimistic about the future.

Ostensibly, she was supposed to be grading papers, but her thoughts kept turning to Cody, so she was distracted when the door to her office opened. She looked up, and a young man stood in the doorway. She didn't recognize him from her classes, but she assumed he was one of her students. "I'm sorry, but I have open office hours on Tuesday and Thursday from two to four. I'm not available right now for discussions."

She wanted to reprimand him for not knocking, but she was in too good of a mood to let someone's ill manners ruin it. The things Cody had done to her last night... She cleared her throat, forcing her attention back to the young man when he stepped into the office and closed the door behind himself. She frowned at him. "You'll have to come back later."

He stared at her, an odd look in his eyes. It was one of longing, if she had to identify it, though not the romantic sort. He seemed to want something, but she had no idea what that could be. Using her pen, she pointed to the door he had just closed. "Please let yourself out, and remember to knock next time when you come back during open office hours. Tuesdays and Thursdays from two to four," she reminded him sternly.

"You don't recognize me, do you, Dr. Barnes?"

She let out a long sigh, preparing to deal with an irritated student. Perhaps she had given him a grade he considered unfair last semester or the semester before that, and he hadn't bothered to follow up until now, as he hovered on the verge of graduation. It was the best theory she could hypothesize on short notice.

She tapped the pen against the desk impatiently. "No, I'm afraid I don't."

"I was on Dr. Sig's team on the island. Your group kept beating him to all the good finds."

She studied him a little closer, still not really recognizing him, though perhaps his face was vaguely familiar. "I think I remember you, or at least I've seen you around the island." Their sites had been separated by at least half a mile, so they hadn't interacted very often with Dr. Sig's group, so she really couldn't recall if she'd seen the kid before or not. "What may I do for you?"

"Dr. Sig was so angry when you kept getting all the good finds. He used to rant and rave about it, and then he'd blame us for not finding more important and significant artifacts."

She eyed him with confusion. "I see. It doesn't surprise me from what I know of Dr. Sig. He probably planned to plunder and sell whatever he could melt down into gold. His behavior must have been difficult to handle, but I'm not certain how it's relevant to me."

He smiled at her as he walked closer, leaning against the edge of her desk instead of taking the seat across from it. He was clearly there for the duration, paying no mind to the fact that she was busy and trying to get rid of him. "I just thought you might find that funny. Some of us had a good laugh every time you found something terrific, and he went and got a little more unhinged."

At the word unhinged, she frowned as comprehension started to dawn. "Is Dr. Sig the one who broke into my office and home and Dr. Deceric's office? Is he the one who killed Eli and injured Glenda?" Her irritation rose rapidly.

He shook his head. "No, that wasn't Dr. Sig. That was me."

ear gripped her suddenly, and she held onto the pen so tightly that it snapped in her hand. She cursed at the sharp shards of plastic as she dropped it on the desk and reached for a tissue to blot the bleeding from the small wound. "Why would you do that?"

"I might be just a postgrad student, but I know the importance of the finds you made, particularly the scepter of Inanna."

She arched her brow. "Good for you for paying attention in class, but I'm still not certain why you've come to me. You must know that I'm not going to ignore the fact that you broke in to my personal space and injured someone. Besides, you're the one with the scepter, according to Glenda."

He reached into his pocket and pulled out an old book, one that had been bound in animal hide and had seen many better days. She instantly recognized it as the book she had found during the excavation of the site. She frowned at him. "What are you doing with that?"

"I'm studying it. It appears to have belonged to a high

priestess of Inanna. It details their daily lives, offerings for the goddess, and most importantly, how to call Inanna to possess a human host."

She scoffed. "Don't be ridiculous. That was based on mythology that's five thousand years old. You should be well educated, or at least educated enough to know what nonsense that is."

He shrugged in an airy fashion. "Perhaps, but I like to keep an open mind. I have everything I need to perform the ritual, so I don't see any reason not to at least try."

She eyed him skeptically as a frisson of fear raced up her spine. Knowing the things he'd already done left her terrified of him despite his lack of threatening demeanor at the moment.

"The ritual calls for the scepter, the book, a sacrifice, and a host."

She shuddered slightly when he used the word sacrifice. "I think you should go now. As I've already explained, my office hours are on Tuesdays and Thursdays, and I'm busy with other work at the moment."

He gave her a look that was almost filled with pity. "I'm afraid I can't do that, Dr. Barnes. You're a key ingredient to the ritual."

She attempted levity, hoping to get through to him and burst the bubble of delusion surrounding him. "I don't see how I could be a critical ingredient to anything. I don't have any ingredients around either for magical spells. Sorry, but I'm fresh out of eye of newt."

He just sighed, as though he felt sorry for her lack of vision. "It's not a magical spell. Or maybe it is. I really don't know what it is, but if it works, it'll be amazing. I'll be rich and famous, and Inanna will have returned."

She tried a different approach. "Are you sure you really want Inanna back? She was the goddess of fertility and love, but she was also the goddess of war, and she was vindictive like most goddesses. You might be her faithful servant one day and end up torn limb from limb the next if you do something to displease her."

He waved a hand in her direction. "Please stop pandering to me, Dr. Barnes. I know you don't believe in the ritual, and I'm not sure I do either, but I see no harm in trying it."

She glared at him. "I see harm in it. I don't particularly feel like being a human sacrifice for your little ritual."

He gave her a small smile, one that was probably meant to be reassuring. "Don't worry, Dr. Barnes. It isn't a sacrifice in that way. It's a blood sacrifice, of a fashion, but from what I can discern, there's no need for you to die."

She eyed him skeptically. "What does that mean then? Do you need some of my blood?"

"In a way. I need you to give me your child, which is a type of sacrifice."

She reared back in shock, instinctively cupping her stomach. "You're out of your mind."

He held up a hand. "Please hear me out. According to the ritual, it requires a willing pregnant woman to sacrifice her child as the human host for Inanna. All I need you to do is agree to give me the child after her birth so I can perform the ritual. I'm not asking for your life."

She didn't know how to handle that request. It was so insane that there were no words for it. She wanted to be cool and logical, to try to reason with him, but she feared he was already far past that point. "I'm not giving you my child. You're absolutely nuts."

He gave her an earnest look. "Can't you see how perfect this is? It's like destiny. You're the one who found the artifact again, and you can have the honor of having Inanna reborn into your child's body."

"It's hardly an honor, and what happens to my child's soul?"

He shrugged. "I don't believe in souls."

She let out a shaky laugh, edged with hysteria. "You believe in some crazy old ritual that's five thousand years old, but you don't believe there might be a spark or essence inside us that makes us who we are? There's a flaw in your thinking." Likely due to complete insanity, but she left that part unuttered. "The answer is no, and I suggest you leave my office before I call the police." Of course she was going to call Detective Strand as soon as she got rid of the young man, but he didn't need to know that.

"I'm not naïve, Dr. Barnes. I know you'll turn me over to the authorities if you aren't willing to make the sacrifice. I guess we just have to do the ritual without one ingredient, which is a willing pregnant woman. I imagine it will still work either way—if it's going to, I mean."

"I said no."

He shook his head, looking almost regretful. "Now who's being naïve? I'm not really asking you, Dr. Barnes. I'm telling you you're going to help me with this, and we're going to leave the school together and find a quieter place to work." He was subtle about it, but he opened his jacket to show her a gun tucked into the belt of his pants. "I don't want it to become anything messy, but you will come with me now." His tone brooked no argument.

Dread filled her, and when he gestured for her to stand up, she was afraid not to comply. She trembled as she took a step away from her desk, whimpering slightly when he put a hand on her arm and anchored her against him.

"You can't do this. It's really wrong. You must know that, even though you aren't thinking clearly. What would your mother think about you trying to steal my baby?"

He shrugged. "I have no idea. She abandoned me at birth, and I was raised in foster care."

That hadn't gone as she had expected, and she swallowed, temporarily rendering herself mute as she searched for a way to get through the young man's delusions. "I'm having boys, you know."

He faltered for a step. "Pardon?"

"I'm pregnant with twins, and they're both boys. It doesn't seem like fate when you look at it that way, does it? I mean, if Inanna had somehow planned all this, wouldn't she have picked a host that was having a single baby girl?"

He seemed to ponder it for a moment, confusion in his expression before he shrugged again. "I'm certain that Inanna will be thankful to be resurrected, and it won't matter to her if she has to share a male body. And this way, there are two in case I do something wrong, and the ritual doesn't work the first time."

Up until that point, she had been at least slightly optimistic that she might get through to him, or find a way to deter him. She realized now that her mistake was thinking he was approaching this logically or rationally at all. He had fixated on the idea of resurrecting a five-thousand-year-old goddess, so clearly he wasn't using his rational brain. She didn't know how to appeal to the side of him that was dominant at the moment, because she didn't speak crazy, so she fell silent.

It wasn't a silence of timidity or being cowed. It was simply a silence of strategy as she tried to think of a way to escape him. She could scream as soon as they hit the quad, but he might shoot her, the twins, and other innocent people. On the other hand, if she allowed herself to be taken somewhere quiet with him, away from any prying eyes, there was no telling what he would try to do. When his little ritual failed, he might finally come to his senses and let her go, or he might decide to kill her to cover his tracks.

"How long do you have to wait to find out if your ritual works? Is it until the baby is born?"

He shook his head. "Not at all. There's another ritual in here for inducing birth, and according to the book, Inanna will quickly grow from a fetus to an adult woman, or man, as the case may be. All we have to do is induce birth, and she'll take care of the rest." His eyes gleamed with sudden surge of excitement. "It probably doesn't even matter that it's a boy. I'm sure Inanna can manipulate the body she's given to become female if she can make it develop from an infant to an adult in a matter of minutes."

Her heart paused for a beat when she realized he planned to induce labor. Even with the growth advantage her babies had as half bear-shifter, they were still far too young to survive outside the womb without major medical intervention. She didn't for one minute believe some mythical goddess was going to be able to possess one of the children and grow into an adult before he could die. If she went with him, he was planning to kill her babies, and probably her too.

That cinched it, and she opened her mouth to scream for help. Instead, a tiny squeak of surprise left her as she saw a bear running their way, a bundle of something in its mouth. It should have been a frightening sight, but she knew immediately it was Cody. She didn't know why he was there, or how he had known to shift into his bear form, but he was there, and she suddenly felt safe again.

Apparently, the young man didn't share her reaction. He saw Cody running toward him, and he started to scream. Cody, in his bear form, was attracting a crowd, and the young man abruptly released her arm as he turned to run away. She wasn't sure if she was surprised or not when Cody continued running after him, temporarily ignoring her. It seemed strange that he didn't pause to check on her, but if he had sensed she was in danger, he would definitely want to deal with whoever had put her there.

She couldn't bring herself to admonish him, or ask him not to go after the young man, because he needed to be locked up. He definitely needed some kind of mental help, and as long as he was free, she and her babies were in danger.

he young man rounded the corridor, with Cody close on his heels. She couldn't see what happened, but she heard the younger one screaming and begging for his life before the roar of the bear drowned it out. A moment later, there was a thud of flesh against the wall, and Jade flinched at the sound. Her mind tried to supply a mental image to accompany what might have made that sound, but she quickly shut down the idea. She didn't want to know, and she certainly didn't want to see. For the first time in a few weeks, a surge of nausea assailed her, and she nearly lost the battle before her stomach calmed after several deep breaths.

Less than a minute after they had disappeared around the corner, Cody walked out and headed her way. He wore simple jogging pants and a t-shirt, and she recognized them as the bundle that had been in his mouth when his bear had raced by. She wondered if there had been any witnesses to what had happened in the hallway, and then she wondered what exactly had happened. She would have to find out the details later, but for now, she was content just to throw herself into his arms when he came rushing toward her, sweeping her into a hug.

As he pulled back, his eyes gleamed with a conspiratorial light, and he raised his voice loud enough for several people in the vicinity to hear, "Am I the only one who just saw a bear running through the campus?"

The hallway was suddenly filled with chatter as people responded to the question, speaking both to Cody and each other. Under the discordant hum of conversation, she pulled Cody to the side, lowering her voice. "What happened to that kid?"

He frowned. "He's still alive. I don't how I knew, but I could tell you were in danger. I tore out of class right in the middle of a lecture, paused just long enough to grab a spare set of clothes, and came running to find you. When I saw him holding you, I could tell you didn't want to be there, and the bear took over. My suit is in tatters all over the quad, but I don't think anyone actually saw me shift, so we should be fine."

"So you left him alive then?" She wasn't entirely certain she was happy about that, though she understood the necessity. It was really for the best not to kill him, and even if he had seen Cody shift, if he was still conscious, no one was likely to believe him in light of all his other mental problems.

He nodded, looking regretful. "I figured it was for the best. I don't know the circumstances, but I just could sense you were in danger."

She put a hand on her stomach. "Not just me. I'll tell you all about it later, but right now, I just want to sit down and let you rub my feet."

He laughed as he took her hand to lead her back to her office. "I think I've created a monster there."

She shrugged. "Perhaps."

They returned to her office, and he closed the door,

spending a moment to make a phone call to Detective Strand before turning back to her. "There will be questions to deal with, but Jason will keep it discreet, if possible. In the meantime, while we're waiting for him to arrive, I think I owe you a foot massage."

She nodded. "I think you do."

They sat on the couch in her office, and she slipped her feet out of the sandals she had worn, happily able to free her feet that much faster. He really was gifted with his foot massages, and after the trauma she'd endured, she considered herself lucky to have someone to give her one. "Would you like me to tell you all about it now?"

He nodded, his expression remaining neutral, and he remained unspeaking as she poured out the details. The only indication he gave of his intense anger was the occasional over-tightening of his hand on her foot, which made her yelp once or twice. He always gentled his touch immediately, and he seemed calm and collected when she was done.

"I should have killed him."

She shook her head. "No, you did the right thing. The kid is clearly unbalanced, and maybe now he'll get some help."

"Where's the scepter?"

"On him presumably."

Cody looked troubled. "What if?"

She found him. "What if what?"

He shrugged. "What if he's right? What if there's even the slightest chance that the ritual would work?"

She was troubled by the question. "Are you suggesting we try it?"

He looked disgusted by the idea. "Of course not. I just wonder if maybe we should get rid of the scepter and the book. Maybe they were buried there for good reason. Even if they weren't, if there are any other unhinged individuals out there who might buy into it, another pregnant woman and her baby could be endangered someday."

She shook her head. "You're letting your imagination get away with you." They fell into silence after that for the next few minutes as they waited the detective's arrival. Despite herself, she began to wonder, too.

What if?

EPILOGUE

*W*aves lapping on the shore offered soothing background music provided by Mother Nature as she cuddled closer to Cody. There was a chill in the summer evening air, and she was thankful for the fire to keep them warm. They laid together on a sleeping bag, not bothering with the tent.

They had been married earlier that afternoon at Bear Island, where Cody's family lived. Her parents had been too frail to make the trip from the Caribbean, where they were retired, and she hadn't been surprised. Hurt, maybe, but unsurprised.

That wedding had been a traditional human ceremony, and then they had taken a boat to another small island nearby to celebrate their honeymoon. It wasn't her idea of luxury, but she could certainly handle a night or two under the stars with her new husband as he prepared to solidify their union in his people's traditional way.

En route to the island, they had dropped the scepter and the book overboard into the Strait of Juan de Fuca. Perhaps it was paranoid and superstitious, and she felt a strong pang of guilt at denying the world access to the historical artifacts, but she been unable to fully convince herself that it was all nonsense.

Once the idea that someone might believe strongly enough in the superstition to harm a woman and child had taken hold, she'd been paranoid about it, too. It didn't have to be her babies that were targeted. If the journal and the scepter fell into the wrong hands, any nut job anywhere could decide to attack a pregnant woman and try to resurrect Inanna in her infant.

It was too big of a risk, even if it was completely bogus. Someone could be seriously injured in the process, if not killed. That had been more important than preserving the artifacts for display in a museum. Aside from poor Dr. Deceric's death, there had been no permanent damage so far due to the items.

She hadn't been injured, Glenda had fully recovered from her injury, and Stuart Vine, the person who had attacked her, was currently an inpatient at a local mental hospital. He had a history of schizophrenia and hearing voices, but his parents had been unable to get him the help he needed until he had escalated to the point of violence. At least that facet had worked out for the best, she supposed, and she'd had no other negative emotions besides that flash of guilt as she had dropped the items into the water.

Now, she completely turned her thoughts from that and to her new husband. His hands had been busy roaming over her, and she realized he'd stripped her from the waist up. That was an unfair advantage on his part, so she set about righting the situation, until they were missing an equal amount of clothing.

He rolled her onto her back, gentle with her burgeoning stomach. The twins would arrive within three weeks, and she was nervous about the idea, but also excited. She was actually having a boy and a girl, having just told Stuart it was two boys in an attempt to distract him. They had learned the genders at their last appointment, which had been her first with a new obstetrician, who was also a cheetah-shifter. The babies were thriving, and so was she under Cody's gentle care.

Now, she was thriving under his sensual touch as he kissed her while his hand stroked her body. She moaned softly when he bent his head to lick her nipple before sucking on the turgid peak. She was sensitive there, and his touch was light, but satisfying enough to almost make her orgasm. It was ridiculous how easy he could manipulate her body, and she appreciated his masterful skills.

They managed to rid each other of the rest of their clothing between giggles and kisses, and when he moved between her parted thighs, his cock ready to claim her, she bent her head back to offer her shoulder for him as well. She knew he was going to completely claim her tonight in his way, the way of his people. She had no hesitation, aside from a little anxiety about whether it would hurt, though he'd assured her it wouldn't.

She forgot her concerns as their bodies joined, and he began to thrust carefully into her. She was soon on the verge of coming, and she clung tightly to him. Just as the first shockwave of her orgasm started, Cody bent his head and bit her on the shoulder. There was no pain at all. Rather, it caused a surge in arousal that elevated her orgasm to new heights. She'd never come so hard or intensely in her life, and she clung to him as her only anchor when the rest of her world was swept away.

Cody's shaft hardened more inside her, and he twitched before he found his own release, spilling into her. His teeth remained in her skin for a moment longer as they held each other and rode out the culmination of their joining. Afterward, they lay together in a panting, gasping heap. When she could breathe and think again, she turned her head to look at him. "That was amazing."

He grinned, looking kind of cocky. "It was, and it will be like that every time from now on."

She let out a mock groan. "I think you're going to kill me. I'm going to die from pleasure."

He put his arm around her, hand on her belly, and his expression was serious and gentle. "I'm going to take care of you for the rest of my life and yours. I love you, Jade."

She let out a small breath, temporarily overwhelmed and almost yielding to the threat of crying. They were purely happy tears, but she was afraid they would upset Cody if he saw them fall. After regaining control, she cleared her throat and pressed her lips to his cheek.

When she pulled back, she whispered, "I love you, too," into his ear. It wasn't the first time she'd said it him in the last couple of weeks, but it was the first time she'd said it as both his wife and his mate, and it seemed to hold special meaning. It did for her, too, adding the final seal to their union—one she was certain would last for the rest of their lives.

BONUS EXCERPT: FIGHTING FOR HER BEAR

Maya Coleson moved with the crowd as they poured off the boat, allowing the others to guide her. It was her first time at the event, and she hoped it would be her last.

The crowd stopped moving a few hundred feet from the dock, automatically splitting into three lines. She moved into the closest one, trying to see over the people in front of her to determine why they were standing in line.

After a twenty-minute wait, she discovered why when it was her turn. A hulking behemoth of a man stood before her, a turnstile to his left. It was one of three, and they were attached to seriously scary-looking barbed-wire-topped fences. He was certainly less than friendly when he eyed her. "Betting starts at a thousand bucks, and cash up front." He eyed her closely. "You're new."

She nodded. "This is my first time at the bear fights." Even uttering the words made her feel queasy.

He scowled. "How did you hear about this? It's discouraged to discuss this among others. Who is your referral?"

"James McCoy," she said quickly. She hoped she remembered his last name, or that he had given her the right last name. He'd sought out the Seattle chapter of Hand & Paw, wanting to report about the bear fights in hopes the group would do something to bring them down.

Unfortunately, when the other members discovered the fights were happening on a private island in the San Juan chain, and it required a good outlay of cash to even step onto the island, they had hesitantly decided not to track the tip.

Maya was more stubborn, and she was blessed with a healthy bank account, so she'd pursued it on her own when no one expressed an interest in joining her.

The guard/bookie grimaced. "I hope you're better at paying your debts than McCoy is."

She mumbled something as she removed a stack of cash from the pocket of her hoodie. She passed it to him and moved toward the turnstile.

He put up a hand, blocking her way. She couldn't help noticing his hand was as large as her face. "Which bear?"

"Rampage." She picked randomly after glancing at the board posted behind the entrance, each name handwritten in chalk. She had no interest in profiting from these fights. She just wanted to bring them down.

The guard inclined his head. "You like a sure thing, huh?" He made the comment as he passed over a small slip. "Don't lose that, or you can't collect your winnings."

"If I win," she said inanely, assuming it was the sort of conversation he'd expect her to have.

He smirked. "You bet on Rampage. It's practically a sure thing. The boss is gonna have to mix it up soon, or people will get bored with the same bear always winning."

Taking her slip of paper, which she pushed into the pocket of her hoodie, she moved through the turnstile and followed the pathway ahead of her. Her destination was obvious, even though she wasn't moving in tandem with the crowd now. There was a large wooden structure ahead of them, and she moved toward it.

Two guards stood on either side of the metal doors that were currently pushed open. She didn't make eye contact as she slipped through the doorway and into the crowd, making sure she'd blended in with the others before she took a moment to evaluate the situation.

Looking over the throng, Maya quickly ascertained she was one of the few women present. She was certainly the only one without a male companion, and none of the other women wore jeans and a hoodie. They were all glammed up in a variety of dresses that could've passed for business-casual to a formal event.

The few other women all looked bored, and most were hanging from the arm of considerably older men. They looked like they wanted to be anywhere but here.

She knew the feeling, but she forced herself to remain where she was, off to the side, with a clear view of the arena below.

Perhaps "ring" would've been a better choice of words, she decided as she looked down over the railing that blocked people from falling into the hole dug into the floor several feet below. It was lined with concrete, and she winced when she saw the blood stains that probably couldn't be completely removed. It was a utilitarian space, but knowing what it was used for made her stomach churn with nausea.

She gripped the rail in front of her for support, remembering abruptly when she was five years old and had stood in a similar position. That time, she'd ended up okay, though traumatized. She hoped this time, she could skip the trauma and emerge from the fighting arena unscathed.

Physically, she was in no danger, and she was no longer five years old, so she was smart enough not to climb the railing, but emotionally, she was certain that whatever she witnessed this evening would haunt her forever.

It took another twenty minutes for everyone who'd been on the boat to pass through security and place their bets, and by the time a whistle sounded, indicating the fight would begin soon, the building was packed. It was too crowded, hot, and noisy, all of which contributed to her nausea.

She clung tensely to the rail when another whistle sounded, and two doors in the arena below opened at the same time.

At first, no bears emerged, but then two lumbered out, both from different doors. She gasped softly when she saw the two guards behind the larger grayish-black bear, both holding cattle prods they used to force the bear to move forward.

She wanted to steal the prods and turn them on the guards, but she forced herself to remain still.

The little lapel camera she'd arranged earlier, which looked like a golden bear pin, was perfectly arranged to get most of the ring below. Maya slipped her hand into her hoodie pocket and pressed a button on the tiny remote in there.

She'd practiced the move multiple times, so her thumb immediately found the round button that began the recording. She pushed it as she watched the bears circle each other warily for a moment.

Initially, the bears didn't do anything. They just stood there, both looking kind of defeated. It was an odd word, but she couldn't think of a better one to describe the poor, sad animals below. They clearly didn't want to be there, and who knew what kind of suffering they'd already endured at the hands of the sadistic monsters?

The crowd was starting to grumble when the bears didn't fight, and she watched with surprise and a touch of horror when one of the guards came back to the door, holding a large-barrel rifle.

She clamped a hand over her mouth when he lined up a shot, wondering if she was going to see the poor animals murdered for failure to fight. Instead, the guards shot them with something, and she thought it might've been a tranquilizer dart, though that made no sense.

A moment later, she discarded that notion when the bears' demeanor changed rapidly. They lost the weary, defeated postures and both became aggressive. The hairs on their backs stood up, and their ferocious growls filled the air.

She forced herself to stand still and keep recording, but she couldn't look when the bears crashed into each other, standing on their hind paws and swiping at each other with their front paws. There was more growling and a cry of pain, but she didn't open her eyes.

Maya endured the horrible sounds for the next few minutes, knowing she needed ample video to turn over to the authorities, but when one let out a low, keening cry that was laced with agony, she shuddered and turned away.

With her hand in her pocket, she turned off the camera and slipped through the crowd, intent on getting outside to breathe in fresh air and escape the sounds and sights of the poor bears being forced to fight each other.

As she edged around the crowd, she had the sensation of eyes on her. With a frown, she looked around, before looking up, as though her gaze had been drawn that way by a magnet. She was disconcerted to see another tier above them, and the setup was certainly more elegant than the main audience floor.

There were only two people sitting in the box, with guards flanking them from behind, and she guessed they must be the fight organizers. Rage swept through her, but the daunting sight of four guards behind the men kept her from doing anything rash, like confronting them.

She quickly realized the one watching her was the younger one. He was probably in his late-thirties, and he had dirty blond hair cropped close to his head, along with a sparse beard that would've looked better if he'd just shaved it all off. She couldn't tell his eye color from here, but his gaze was certainly locked on her.

She almost shuddered when he sent her a flirtatious smile and waved a hand in her direction. Feigning shyness, she dipped her head and looked away, intent on escaping the structure as quickly as possible.

When she stepped outside, the cool breeze from the Strait of Juan de Fuca tickled her hair and caressed her face, the sharp tang of salt in the sea air helping restore her calm and soothe her nausea. Her mind tried to imagine what was happening in the ring below, but she shut down that thought as soon as it could form. She really didn't want to know.

She was aware of the guards watching her, so she stayed in their sight without looking at them as she waited for the fight to end. Less than thirty minutes later, the crowd started spilling out, all heading back to the boat. She mingled with them, not breaking away until she was far enough from the structure to feel like the guards wouldn't immediately see her do so.

It was a dark night, with only a fingernail moon to guide her, but that worked in her favor, even though it slowed her down. Between the lack of moonlight and her dark clothing, she blended in pretty well, she hoped. To be on the safe side, she tightened her hoodie around her head, not wanting any of her blonde hair to escape and be visible in the darkness.

She knew she'd have to hurry, because the last thing she wanted was to miss the boat and be stuck on this island for two days, when the next fights occurred. Still, she couldn't leave without knowing the living conditions of the bears, and perhaps finding out how they'd fared physically after the fight.

She assumed there were more than two bears being held in captivity, and she briefly entertained the idea of sneaking into their enclosure and freeing them all, and then allowing the bears to run free. Ultimately, she discarded the plan. It wasn't because she was worried about innocent people getting hurt. There was no one innocent on the island except for the bears and herself. She was here for a noble purpose, not to see two suffering animals rip each other to shreds and win money on the outcome.

She also wasn't eager to be torn apart by the bears, and she couldn't imagine a scenario where she could free them and get clear of their path in time to avoid becoming a casualty.

The island was bigger than she'd thought upon approaching from the boat, and as she moved past the fighting structure in a wide arc, her eyes widened at the sight of a huge mansion a few hundred yards ahead of her. It was well-lit, at least enough to allow her to see the details.

The large, off-white structure dominated the area around it, and though she didn't know architecture styles very well, the entire building reminded her of a hacienda one might see in Texas, as a holdover from pre-Civil War days, or in Central and South America. It was an incongruous sight on an island near Seattle, but she didn't have time to indulge her curiosity.

She certainly wasn't approaching the house anyway. It was clearly a private residence and likely belonged to the two horrible people she'd seen in the private box, the architects of the suffering of the bears on this island.

With that reminder, she turned away from the huge house and moved deeper into the island. She could feel the seconds ticking past in a desperate rhythm, certain she was running out of time to make it back to the boat. Even knowing that, she couldn't force herself to turn around and head back that way. Not yet.

She heard the bear enclosure before she saw it. She could hear the moans of anguish, and the occasional growling sound. She was startled by how human the bears sounded, which made her even angrier that they were being exploited this way. They were sensitive, intelligent creatures, and to know they were being forced to fight each other for sick people's amusement sent rage spiraling through her.

She took several deep breaths in an attempt to keep it in check as she eased closer to the enclosure. She was just in time to see the man who'd given her a flirtatious grin step into sight.

She counted at least five cages holding bears, though only two were occupied at the moment. She immediately recognized the big gray-black bear from the fight, along with his slightly smaller companion, who was a golden-brown color. They both laid in their cages, looking exhausted and defeated again.

In shock, she watched as the man wielded a rifle similar to the one the guard had used to shoot the bears at the beginning of the fight. She was still trying to process why they would need to do that, assuming it was some sort of tranquilizer, when the bears seemed to melt in front of her. She let out a small gasp before clapping a hand over her mouth to keep in further unwanted sounds, trying to figure out what she was seeing.

Her thumb automatically hit the record button on the remote even as her mind struggled to process the transformation of bears to human men. She shook her head, disbelief coursing through her. She certainly couldn't have seen what she thought she had. Could she?

But how could she doubt the evidence before her? The bears were gone, replaced by two lethargic men who lay in their cages.

The closest one to her had a perfect physique, with thick muscles, a lean waist, and clearly defined abdominal muscles. He was rough, smeared with blood and covered with dirt, and his black hair was overgrown and shaggy, but in the lighting provided by the lamps overhead, she saw it was still a thick mass of ebony.

When he was cleaned up, his hair no doubt shone with a hint of blue in the black. Right now, it was matted and filthy, and there was no shine anywhere.

Pity swept through her, and though she wasn't certain what was happening, she still couldn't stand by and watch it. She was considering moving forward and knocking out the guy with the gun somehow so she could free the humans when a hand fell on her shoulder. She froze, letting out a small cry of dismay as she turned to look up at the guard who'd taken her bet. She tried to force a shaky smile, but she was certain all she did was grimace at him as fear and anger warred for supremacy.

"Move," he said in more of a grunt than a word. His hand remained clamped on her shoulder as he shoved her forward, her petite, curvy frame no match for his larger, harder body.

Fear consumed her, and it was difficult to breathe, so she forced herself to focus on doing so, slightly controlling her anger and terror by slowing down her breathing.

Her breathing exercises did little to keep her calm when the security guard pushed her into the other man's line of sight. Her stomach clenched with dread when she saw the male interest in his eyes, indicating he wanted her. That was the last thing she wanted, but she struggled to hide her revulsion at his flirtatious smirk.

"What's this?" he asked the guard, though he didn't look away from her.

"She was snooping over there in the shadows, and you know Señor Calderon's rule. If they see something, the gamblers don't leave the island."

A chill ran through her at the words, though she was unsurprised by that rule. Common sense dictated it would have to exist, because he wouldn't want word of his illegal bear-fighting enterprise to leak out.

A quick glance at the two men in the cages reminded her there was something far more sinister at work here than simply forcing two bears to fight each other. That was bad enough, but she couldn't fathom the depths of depravity occurring on this island.

"What're you doing snooping out here, young lady?" The man with the rifle asked the question sternly, but there was disquieting hunger in his gaze as it slipped over her, taking in her appearance from head to toe. "Were you looking for me?"

Briefly, she considered playing into that notion, but realized it could quickly escalate out of control. She had a feeling flirting with this man would be even worse than admitting the full truth of why she was here. The slightest sign of encouragement on her part would probably set in motion a series of events she couldn't and didn't want to face. Instead, she cleared her throat. "I'm sorry. I was just curious about the bears. I wanted to know what happened to them after the fight."

He was still leering at her, but the hint of wariness had faded. "You seem like a tender little thing, having to leave the fight at the midway point." His brown eyes narrowed slightly. "Which begs the question why you'd come somewhere like this to start with?"

"I was curious." It was a lame excuse, but she hoped he'd

buy it. He seemed to want to, so she forced herself to give him a smile while she fluttered her eyelashes at him. "It's one of my biggest flaws. I just want to know everything."

"How'd you end up on our island?"

The guard behind her spoke up for the first time since he'd explained why he brought her to the other man. "James McCoy referred her."

The man grimaced. "I hope you aren't as unreliable as your friend. He still owes Señor Calderon quite a bundle."

She shook her head, quickly realizing just why James had brought the bear-fighting ring to Hand & Paw's attention. It had nothing to do with concern for the bears' welfare. He was simply hoping they would gather enough intel to interest the authorities and spur them to action. He probably thought their group would be the catalyst to bring down the people on this island, thereby negating his debt.

She'd previously admired him for speaking up about the problem, and she'd believed him when he'd said he had stumbled onto the situation while going with a friend to what he thought was going to be a regular underground fight between two willing participants. Now, she quickly lost any hint of admiration for the other man.

"He's not a friend. He's someone I met once or twice, that's all."

"So he isn't your boyfriend?" asked the other man.

She was disturbed by the gleam of interest, and she quickly shook her head. She didn't want to dwell on anything that reminded the guy of dating or sex. "Who are you?" she asked, trying to change the subject quickly.

"I'm Dr. Elgin Stone, but I think that question belongs to me. Who are you?"

"Maya Cole—" She broke off quickly, realizing she shouldn't give him her real name. Too bad she hadn't had that epiphany before she started speaking hers out of habit.

At least she hadn't given him her full last name, though it'd be easily discovered if they bothered to investigate her. She'd left her identity behind at the university, but she had her phone on her, so she doubted they'd have much trouble figuring out who she was if they took her things.

"Maya, I'm afraid this may be a situation where curiosity killed the cat." He sounded regretful, even as he leered at her breasts, though he clearly couldn't have seen much of anything through the oversized hoodie.

She gulped, trying to clear the lump in her throat. "You're going to kill me?" She tried to go for a disbelieving, almost girlish tone, but she was certain it fell flat. She just couldn't seem to force herself to flirt with the creepy man in front of her, especially when he was talking about murdering her.

He shook his head. "That isn't my call, sweetheart. If it were, I'm certain we could find other uses for you. That's up to Señor Calderon, though. He owns the island, and he's the one who makes the final decisions on what to do with people like you."

She arched a brow. "People like me?" she repeated, her lips numb as the implications of being discovered started to sink in. Up until that point, she'd been optimistic she could talk her way out of this, simply by building on the attraction the doctor had for her.

Knowing there was another person entering the equation had robbed her of any confidence. Her gaze started around, and she saw the man in the cage behind Stone.

He looked bewildered and was clearly drugged, but when their gazes met, his eyes widened, and his nostrils flared. He jerked upright for just a moment, growling something incomprehensible, though he was in his human form.

Those words reverberated inside her skull, sounding too fantastical to believe. Even though she'd seen the transition with her own eyes, she was still half-hoping for a different explanation, one that was reasonable and didn't involve the reality of a bear turning into a human.

"Take her to Señor Calderon," said the doctor, his regret visible.

Her fearful gaze hadn't moved from the human's, and he growled again, clearly making an effort to get to his feet. She had the strangest certainty he was trying to intercede to save her, but the poor man was clearly in no condition to do so. Whatever they'd pumped into him had left him incapacitated and drugged.

Pity swelled in her, but she forced it back. It was a nonproductive emotion, and if she was going to pity anyone, she should probably pity herself.

Her odds of outliving the man in the cage behind her seemed fairly grim.

ABOUT THE AUTHOR

Paranormal romance author Aria Chase combines her fascination with the occult and her undying love for happily ever after to create steamy shifter reads that are perfect for devouring in one night.

Follow Aria on Booksprout for access to Advance Review Copies, giveaways and more!

Stay in touch:

www.ariachase.com

ariachase@ariachase.com

ALSO BY ARIA CHASE

Emerald City Shifters

Bearly Breathing

Polar Bond

The Bear's Secret Baby

Fighting For Her Bear

Bought By A Bear

Sundown Wolves

Temptation

Reparation

Distraction